AWAY FROM KEYBOARD COLLECTION

PROTECTING HIS TARGET

PATRICIA D. EDDY

PROLOGUE

Zephyr

MY BACK AND SHOULDERS ACHE, and I drum my gloved fingers on the rickety, stained table. Six hours ago, I wiped down the entire apartment, intending to be gone by sunset. But hacking isn't always fast—or easy—even for me, and my anxiety is on high alert now that it's after midnight.

Everything I care about in this world is carefully arranged in my backpack. A picture of my brother and me when we were just five and eight—before Papa disappeared—the tiger's eye ring he left on my pillow the day he vanished, my multi-tool, and three pairs of thick wool socks. When everything else in my world sucks ass, a warm, dry pair of socks are a godsend.

The rest of the items I acquired during my three-week stay in the Netherlands were tossed into the building incinerator this morning. Clothes, a couple of books, an extra pillow and blanket. Gone. Reduced to ashes. Like my reputation. And my life if I don't get my ass moving.

I always travel light. One bag. Less than ten pounds—

without my computer, anyway. Speed has saved me before, and I can't risk being weighed down.

The code on the screen blurs with my exhaustion, and I double-check that my wool hat is still firmly in place. It stops me from leaving easily traceable DNA, but it also gives me a headache. Pinching the bridge of my nose, I breathe in while I count to four, hold for seven, and exhale for a full eight seconds. Amazingly, this little trick to drive stress away works every time, and some of the tension holding my head in a vise fades away.

Next to the laptop, my phone screen lights up.

Nora: He found me. Came to my office. I had to drive around for hours before I went home to make sure he wasn't following me.

Fuck. Thumbing out a quick reply, I will the progress bar on the screen to move faster.

He'll be in jail by morning. Don't talk to anyone. Keep the doors locked. I'll be there in an hour.

She doesn't answer.

"I promise, babe. After tonight, you'll never have to worry about him again."

The next fifteen minutes feel like a century. Until the First Bank of Rotterdam's firewalls crumble to digital dust.

Finding Sem Jassen's accounts and employee records is a breeze now that I'm in. "You little twat. I knew you were dirty. *But this?* This is a freaking garbage dump of filth."

I'd planned to make it look like Nora's abusive ex was embezzling from his employer. Padding a few bank accounts, planting some rather incriminating emails? Piece of cake. Turns out, all I have to do is add a few *embellishments* to his actions before I send all the evidence to the General Intelligence and Security Service.

"You could have kept that Rolls Royce Phantom. And your freedom. But *no*. You had to beat your wife. In front of her kids. I hope you have fun in prison, asshole."

If this were a movie, the dramatic background music would rise to a crescendo any second now. Instead, while I wait for the data to transfer, I grab the arms of the chair and twist, each vertebra in my back popping in sweet, sweet relief. The progress bar taunts me, creeping along at a pace somewhere between geriatric snail and petrified turtle.

"Come on, come on. I was supposed to be long gone by now."

The seconds tick by, and my knee bounces faster and faster. As soon as the zipped files land in my encrypted cloud storage, I sever the connection to the bank and send everything to Dante. He's one of the only people I trust. I gave him a heads up this morning, and he emails me before I shut down the laptop.

Got everything, Zephyr. Jassen will be in custody before 9:00 a.m. Where are you off to next?

Snorting, I send a quick response.

You didn't really think that would work, did you? Gotta go, D. Catch you next time.

Dante is one of the few people who believes I was set up for Jasper Yoden's murder. But since the only family I had planted my blood and prints at the scene, I don't have enough...*credibility* for the AIVD to do anything but put me away for life.

The laptop and power supply slide into a special, padded pocket in the backpack, and I take one last look around the apartment. I'm going to miss this place. The building's half empty, slated to be torn down in a few weeks. The top two floors are deserted, but with five units still occupied, the owner hasn't disconnected the internet hardline. A couple of calls to the right people at Fiber International, and I doubled the speed.

You're welcome, neighbors I've never met and never will. I hope you enjoyed your unlimited Netflix binges.

With the hood of my jacket pulled low over the wool cap, I

slip into the hall. As I close my gloved fingers around the handle of the stairwell door, tiny shards of plaster hit my cheek.

"The next one won't miss," Oliver calls. "Give it up, Zephyr. We have all the exits covered."

Fear snakes cold fingers around my heart, squeezing so hard, I'm not sure I'm still breathing. From the sound of his voice, he's at least a few yards away. I can make it.

"Did I ever tell you why I let you live three years ago?" I ask, turning slightly so he can't see me twist the door handle.

"Because you're not cut out for this business, Zeph." His cold blue eyes bore into me, the silenced pistol steady in his hands. "You made a mistake, and that mistake is going to bring you in. Back to your family. Back where you belong."

"Family?" I laugh to cover the click as the latch bolt disengages from the strike plate. "François will torture me until he gets what he wants, then put a bullet in my brain. In what fucked-up world is that family?"

"Goddammit, Zephyr. Jessica's dead because of you."

"No. Jessica's dead because she was a compassionate, decent human being and François's a sadistic asshole," I fire back.

Oliver's eyes cloud over for a split second, and I yank the door open. Sprinting as fast as I can *up* the stairs—the exits below may be covered, but I always have multiple escape routes —I try not to panic as my brother's pounding footsteps get closer and closer. He always could beat me in a foot race.

"Shit! She's going up!" he shouts. I hope to all that's holy his surprised tone means he and his team didn't expect me to head this way.

The crisp night air slaps my cheeks as I burst onto the roof, but I don't stop, my entire focus on the plywood ramp at the far end. The one I placed there a week ago. The one that should give me enough momentum to carry me to the next building over.

You can make it. It's only two meters. Piece of cake.

Pain rips through my thigh mid-air, and when I land, my left knee buckles, sending me tumbling ass over elbow. I can't stop. Can't think about the fire licking its way down my leg or the sticky warmth plastering my pants to my skin.

Wrestling my gun from the holster, I fire a single, blind shot behind me once I'm on my feet and racing for the fire escape.

Without a silencer, the sound reverberates through the stillness of western Rotterdam after midnight.

Grabbing the railing, I vault from one set of stairs to the next. Each jump takes me lower, and the pain warns me my leg won't last much longer without treatment. My toes make squishing sounds every time I land.

I'm not cold. Don't feel weak or dizzy yet. If Oliver had hit a major artery, I'd be all of those things. If not dead.

Only sparing a quick glance skyward when I reach the ground, I don't see him—or anyone—following me.

Run. Don't look back. Just run.

IN A DARK ALLEY a few blocks from Nora's flat, I strip out of my bloody pants and toss them in the dumpster. "Shit." The gash is deep, but thank God the bullet didn't hit anything vital. It's *mostly* stopped bleeding. A little clotting powder—even though it hurts like a motherfucker—takes care of the rest.

Voices come from the street, and I sink deeper into the darkness to fish a roll of gauze out of my backpack and wrap my leg tightly. Can't stay here for long. I have to keep moving.

Pants. I need a clean pair of pants first. And shoes. Someone's going to notice if I stroll down the sidewalk tracking blood with every step. Even at 2:00 a.m.

By the time I've put myself together, I'm exhausted. I probably need a blood transfusion but I'll have to settle for a protein bar instead.

Shit. I'm out.

Of course. I was supposed to leave the Netherlands two days ago, but then I connected with Nora in an online chatroom, and I couldn't run knowing she was in danger.

A few deep, centering breaths, and I test my weight on my left leg. A little pain, but as long as I concentrate, I can walk without a limp.

The city's quiet this time of the morning. The traffic cameras still capture everything, though, so I keep my head down until I reach Nora's back door.

My gloved hand leaves a red smudge on the wood when I knock, and I quickly scrub it off with my elbow and rub my palms on my thighs. What's a little more blood to clean up once I'm safe?

The two hours I spent weaving through the city, bleeding, constantly looking over my shoulder? Worth it. In a few minutes, Nora will know she and her daughters never have to be afraid again.

"Who is it?" a lightly accented voice asks.

"Nora? It's your guardian angel."

"What's the password?"

Good. She's being smart. "Kansas."

Three separate locks disengage, and the petite woman with straight blond hair peers into the alley. "You're alone?"

"Yes. Can I come in for five minutes? I can't stay. Had a little run in with my former employers a couple of hours ago."

"Yes. Yes, come." Nora steps back into the light and cradles her arm gently.

"Did he hurt you?" My question comes out harsher than I intend, and the woman shrinks back against her sink. "Dammit. I'm sorry. I...I should have been faster. AIVD will have him in custody by 9:00 a.m. tomorrow, and he'll never bother you or the girls again."

Nora angles a glance up the stairs. The two teenagers—

from her first marriage—had to witness their stepfather's abuse on more than one occasion, but thank God he never laid a hand on them.

With a wince, I drop to one knee and start digging through the backpack for my oilskin bag. Waterproof, practically indestructible, it's the only place I trust for my most important paperwork.

Unzipping the pouch, I spread the contents over Nora's counter. Three new passports and a prepaid credit card. "You said he refused to return your passports when you separated? Well, these are all completely legit, ready for you to move back to England—if you want."

"How did you get these?" Nora asks. "You didn't break into his house, did you?"

"No." Chuckling, I ease myself down onto one of her kitchen chairs and finally, blissfully, remove the tight wool cap over my purple-streaked hair. "Just made friends with a guy in the passport office and had him reissue them."

"And the bank card?" Nora reaches for the plastic rectangle, and her sweater rides up. Fingertip bruises surround her wrist, and I wish I'd been able to confront the jerk myself.

Despite her hesitancy, Nora manages that "mom" stare with ease, and my heart aches. No one's looked at me like that for as long as I can remember. I had a mom once. I think. But hell if I can call up her face. Her voice. Anything about her.

"That's linked to the account I gave you when you hired me. I'm waiving my fee. It's all there. Every one of the ten thousand euros you paid me. That should be enough for you and the girls to make a fresh start. AIVD is probably going to want to interview you once they arrest Sem. So keep that hidden somewhere safe until he's sentenced. But after? Be *happy*, Nora. You deserve it."

Tears tumble down Nora's cheeks, and she reaches out like she wants to hug me, but I don't do touch. Not like that. "Gotta go. Just promise me you'll take care of the girls and...I don't know..." I back toward her door and grin. "Do something fun. I hear dying your hair can really change your whole personality." Tucking a lock of bright purple behind my ear, I give her a little wave before I slip out into the night.

The exhaustion makes every step feel like I'm walking through wet sand, but I can't rest. Not until I've put at least two hundred kilometers between me and François's men—including my brother. I don't know how they tracked me, but once I've found a new safe house, I need to find out.

My life could have ended tonight, and while I've lived with the constant threat of capture, torture, and death for almost four years, I'm not ready to die. Not until I find the only other person in the world with evidence against the Strauss Cartel.

And stop them from hurting anyone else, ever again.

—————

Ronan

Rapping four times on Dax's door, I glance around Second Sight's offices. The halls are quiet three days before Thanksgiving. Marjorie hung lights in the break room, and every day this week, baskets of pumpkin muffins have appeared next to the coffee machine.

"Come in, Ronan," Dax calls.

I'll never get used to the emptiness of Dax's space. All the other offices have at least *some* kind of personal touch. A photograph, a plant...even Ella keeps a *Totoro* plush toy next to her monitor and she's about the least sentimental person I've ever met.

Dax? Nothing.

Closing the door behind me, I try to control my heart rate. My boss is the most observant man on the planet, despite being

8

mostly blind, and showing fear? That's not going to help me. As soon as I take a seat in one of his visitor chairs, my palms turn clammy, and I rub them on my thighs.

"Are you expecting a firing squad?" he asks, staring right at me.

How does he do *that?*

"Maybe."

His dry laugh isn't reassuring in the least. Skimming his fingers over the top of the desk, he finds a beige envelope and holds it out to me. "Your bonus check."

Bonus check?

"Since when did you start givin' out bonuses?" I don't open the thing. Not with the way he's looking at me. Like he can see right through me.

"Always have. Once we promote someone from junior investigator to full associate."

My mouth goes dry, and the envelope slips from my hand, floating to the ground. Grateful for the moment to get myself together, I retrieve it, then swallow hard. I should have brought a cup of tea with me. Water. Whiskey. Anything to distract me from this envelope in my hand.

"Nothin' to say?" Dax asks, the hint of a Southern drawl not softening his tone a bit.

Get yourself together, mate. You're making an idiot of yourself.

"Thank you? I wasn't sure—after what happened in Edgewater—if you were going to keep me on."

His brows shoot up, true surprise obvious in his expression. "Fuck," he mutters. "Ronan, you took a bullet from a professional mercenary and survived."

"I let a group of civilians take me down first. Did you forget about that part? Mik was in trouble, and I couldn't get past a security guard and five guys waitin' for a tour of the Smithsonian."

"Six against one?" Dax shakes his head. "No one in this

office could count on beating those odds. You kept your cool, let Austin know what was goin' on, and stalled long enough for him and Trev to get there."

"And then I got shot." Rubbing my side, the wound not completely healed, I shiver at the memories. Burning pain. Blood cooling on my skin. Fear that the bullet had hit something vital. Something that couldn't be fixed with a few stitches, a pint of O Positive, and a handful of painkillers.

Dax leans back in his chair, pulls off his glasses, and pinches the bridge of his nose. I'm about to ask him if he's all right when he sets the dark frames on his desk. "Every single person in this office with the exception of Vasquez and Marjorie has been shot, stabbed, beaten up, or tortured." He shakes his head and laughs. Actually laughs. "I should probably arrange for some more advanced hand-to-hand combat and evasion classes. That's not exactly a ringing endorsement for my leadership."

"No class would have stopped me from taking a bullet at the Smithsonian. Fucker drew down on me half a second after I came around the corner."

He stares at me—not that I have any idea how he can possibly know right where my eyes are—and I curse under my breath. "Fine. I didn't fuck up as badly as I thought."

"No. You didn't. Goin' to open that envelope? Or just crush it to death?"

I'm clutching the damn thing so hard, my fingers ache, and the paper crinkles softly. Forcing myself to relax, I lift the flap and pull out the check. "Fuck me. Dax, this is too much."

"It's been a good year," he says. "Ripper made a few investments that paid off twenty times over, we split a tidy sum with Pritchard after the mess in Zurich, and now that we've finished the merger with Hidden Agenda..." Dax shrugs. "Second Sight is a family, Ronan. We take care of our own."

I don't have a response. Not one Dax will accept anyway. I

don't fit in here. Never have. Probably why I've spent three years as backup. The job with Pritchard was the closest I've come to my own assignment, and even if I didn't *completely* fuck it up, no one would call it a brilliant success.

"Evianna and I are headed to Seattle tomorrow," Dax says, saving me from the awkward silence. "Cara and West are teaming up to cook a feast for Thanksgiving. There's plenty of room on the plane."

Is he...inviting me to Thanksgiving dinner? "Dax—"

"You don't have to socialize. Much," he says, the corner of his mouth twitching into what might almost be a smile.

"I'm still knackered from my brother's wedding. Haven't had a full night sleep since I got back."

In truth, I've slept like a feckin' baby since I returned from Ireland. But Thanksgiving in Seattle? Pretending to be part of this family? I can't do it. Not now.

"I'm still on Zurich time. So's Austin. Got an excuse that *isn't* total bullshit?" Dax crosses his arms over his chest and arches his brows. "If you don't want to go, that's your choice, Ronan. But don't lie and make me regret giving you that promotion."

Fuck me.

Trying not to twist the envelope so hard I tear the check in half, I look Dax in the eyes. I know he can't see me, but the man's echolocation skills are brilliant, and if I stare down at the floor like I want to, he'll know. "I never fit in back home."

"I remember. It's why you came to me askin' for a job." Dax rubs the back of his neck. "I also know you didn't want to go to Dublin for your brother's wedding. What I don't know is why that has any bearin' on you comin' to Seattle."

"The trip was a bloody disaster. I'd be a crap addition to Thanksgiving dinner." Licking my wounds with a pint of whiskey and a large pizza? That sounds a hell of a lot better than trying to make small talk. Or worse. Finding out no one wants to make small talk with me.

"No one's forcing you." Donning his glasses once more, Dax reaches for his cell phone. "Voice Assist: Text Clive. Message reads: 'Ronan's staying in town. We're wheels up at 10:00 a.m. Don't burn the place down while we're gone and take care of your mom and cousin.' Send message."

"So, it's just me and Clive and Ella?" I ask, smoothing the envelope out on my thigh.

"Second Sight's closed until Monday unless someone calls with an emergency. Ella's flying to Cancun in the morning. Clive is bringing his mom home for a couple of days. You want to be alone for the holiday, that's your choice. I spent six Thanksgivings with a bottle of scotch before I met Evianna. But that's no way to live. So if you change your mind, be at Beverly Municipal Airport by 9:30 tomorrow morning."

The dismissal in his tone? Clear as day. Pushing to my feet, I tuck the check into my pocket. "Have a good holiday, Dax. And thanks. You won't regret promotin' me."

"I'd better not."

As I shut the door, a brief pang of regret twists my heart into a knot. Spending Thanksgiving with a family who *wants* me? It's the stuff of my dreams. But I'd do *something* to screw it up, and then? I'd have nothing left but the shattered pieces of too many dreams that will never come true.

CHAPTER ONE

Ronan

A LIGHT SNOW dusts the sidewalks outside the T station, and I tug the collar of my leather jacket higher around my neck. Dax, Trevor, and Ford are due back in the office, and the text message waiting for me when I woke up this morning confirmed I'm getting my first solo assignment.

I'm torn between apprehension and excitement. My whole life, I've played second chair to...well...everyone. The afterthought. Mum never thought of me as "less than," but the rest of the family? There's a reason my brother's wedding was the first time I'd been back to Ireland in years.

The ten-minute walk to Second Sight's offices leaves me invigorated. Maybe I *can* do this. Maybe I *won't* screw this case up. Whatever this case turns out to be.

"Good morning, Ronan." Marjorie greets me with a smile. "How was your Thanksgiving?"

"Quiet." I don't elaborate. If she finds out I spent the holiday alone with a take-and-bake pizza and the Crystal Palace match on my DVR, I'll never hear the end of it. Marjorie's holidays involve dozens of guests without a moment of peace. I made the mistake of going to a Memorial Day cookout my first year in Boston. I still haven't recovered.

"Dax called. He won't be in until nine. Weather delayed their flight from Seattle." She swipes a cloth over the top of her desk—not that I can see a speck of dust on the polished wood—and nods toward the break room. "There are three pecan pies in the fridge. Grab a slice now before Trevor gets here. You know he's going to put at least half a pie away before five."

"Thanks, Marjorie. I'll do that." She hands me a small stack of messages, and I shuffle through them on my way to my office. Nothing requires an immediate response. As one of three junior investigators—along with Vasquez and Tank—I used to juggle multiple cases at once. Grunt work usually. Research. Surveillance. Paying off informants.

The First Bank of Boston is my only active case. They had a block of ten safe deposit boxes all rented in the same week, and their head of security got suspicious.

Wren—Second Sight's hacker and tech genius—tracked all the renters back to two separate shell companies out of Nova Scotia, and now, I get to spend the next few days combing through security footage to identify the men who rented each box.

At my desk with a large slice of pecan pie and a cup of strong tea, I send Wren a quick email to thank her for working over the holiday. Two minutes later, I almost knock over my mug as a video chat window with her name on it flashes on my screen.

"What are you doin' up at this hour?" I ask when the call connects. Fuck me. She looks knackered—and not in a good way.

Wren takes a quick sip of water and grimaces. "Morning sickness. I've been up since four."

"Isn't that supposed to pass by now?" Wren and I aren't close. She moved out to Seattle two years ago to be with Ryker McCabe, Dax's brother in arms, and we only worked together for eight months before that, but she's one of the nicest people I've ever met.

Covering her mouth with her hand, she darts a glance behind her for a brief moment. "Fudgsicles. Thought I was about to hurl again. Sorry. I'm not quite at five months. My doctor isn't worried. Ry, on the other hand..." she rolls her eyes. "At least he finished the nursery and second bathroom so I don't wake him every single time now."

"Jesus, Mary, and Joseph, Wren. Go back to bed! Nothin' you're workin' on for me is as important as takin' care of yourself."

"If I go back to bed now, Pixel will whine until Ry gets up to walk her, and then he'll insist on making me one of his protein-electrolyte-superfood shakes." She shudders, and her little white Maltese sits up and noses her chin. "They're disgusting, even if they do work."

"I won't tell him you said that." Cracking a smile, I take another sip of tea. "So what do you have for me?"

She eases the dog off her lap and starts typing. Within seconds, a file transfer pops up on my screen. "Background information on the murder of Jasper Yoden. Crime scene photos, local police case notes, and a partial file from the General Intelligence and Security Service. The assassination took place in São Paulo, but Yoden was a Belgian citizen, so they're on point for the investigation."

"Who the bloody fuck—sorry—fudgsicles—is Jasper Yoden?" I cringe at my language. Wren doesn't swear, and while she maintains she doesn't care if those around her do, I try to keep things *a little* cleaner when I talk to her.

"Haven't you met with Dax yet?" she asks, her reddish blond brows knitting together.

"No. You didn't hear? Their flight was delayed out of Seattle. He won't be in for another hour."

Her cheeks flush a bright red. "Spitsnacks. Well...um... when he gets in, pretend I never called. Okay? He'll be crushed if he knows I ruined the surprise. And *don't* look at that file until after you talk to him."

A door opens in the background. "Wren? Sweetheart? What are you doing up?"

Ryker McCabe's nearly seven feet tall and currently wearing only a pair of boxer shorts. Fuck. I knew he'd been tortured within an inch of his life in Hell—a system of caves deep in the Hindu Kush—but despite spending several days with the man on mission in Venezuela last year, I had no idea what he'd been through.

"Rice Krispies!" Wren says sharply and reaches for the camera to swivel it away. "I'm on with Ronan."

"Fuck."

Before I can assure Ryker I didn't see—exactly what I saw— his face fills the call window. Long-healed burns cover his left cheek, and his eye doesn't fully open, a scar bisecting the lid.

"If you *ever* breathe a word—"

"About what? You callin' Wren 'sweetheart'? I'll take your secret to the grave." I rub my hands on my thighs under my desk. Even more than three thousand miles away, Ryker terrifies me. Wren's complete opposite in every way, he and Dax can command a room—or an army—without saying a word.

He stares at me for another few seconds, then nods and his voice fades, "We're getting an 'on call' light."

Wren laughs, a musical, happy sound as she readjusts the camera, then presses her hand to her stomach. "I have to eat something soon or I'll be in a world of hurt." A blender whirrs in the background, and she sighs. "I didn't mean one of your protein-electrolyte-superfood shakes, Ry. Something *normal*. Like...eggs. Or toast. Cereal?"

"Nope. Shake first, then cereal."

Pixel yips several times, and Wren narrows her eyes at me over the call. "Remember. You didn't talk to me or *touch* that file. I have to go. Call me if you need help with any of the grunt work once you talk to Dax."

Before I can reply, the call drops. The brief glimpse into wedded bliss leaves me with an ache deep inside. Every word of Wren and Ryker's bickering was filled with such intense love and respect, that baby is going to be the luckiest kid in the whole fucking world.

My phone beeps twice with a message from Dax. *"My office. Five minutes."*

Time to see what this surprise is all about.

RAPPING four times on Dax's door, I only wait two seconds for him to tell me to come in. "Take a seat," he says, his voice gruffer than usual. Behind his tinted glasses, dark circles brace his eyes. Rubbing the back of his neck, he waits for me to sit before he clears his throat. "We didn't land until 4:00 a.m., so I'm going to keep this short." After pressing a button on his keyboard, he continues. "Voice Assist, initiate file transfer. Source folder: Yoden. Destination folder: Ronan."

I pull out my tablet and tap the notification. Photos spread across the device. A body, half-decomposed, unrecognizable as the smiling man on the other side of the screen. "Double-tap to the head, then tossed into the Tietê River missin' both hands? Professional hit."

"Yup. Jasper Yoden, forty-seven years old. He was in São Paulo for his daughter's wedding," Dax says.

"Fuck. And he never made it?"

"He made it. Disappeared somewhere between the hotel and the airport *after* the ceremony." He skims his fingers over his desk until he finds his coffee mug and takes a sip. "There's not enough caffeine in the world today."

"We can do this tomorrow—"

Shaking his head, Dax sets the cup down, removes his glasses, and pinches the bridge of his nose. "Yoden's brother lives in Seattle. He served with Ry and me before we joined the Special Forces, and we ran into each other at a coffee shop the day after Thanksgiving. Spent a couple hours catching up."

Dax isn't what you'd call "a talker." Three years of working with the man, and the longest conversation we had was when he promoted me. A couple of hours catching up? That's got to be a record for him.

He drains the last of his coffee and leans back in his chair. "Maxwell Yoden has been in contact with the General Intelligence and Security Service in Antwerp. Jasper was Belgian, and while the São Paulo police handled the initial investigation, they worked closely with the Belgians. The case officer knows exactly who killed Jasper. Problem is...they haven't been able to find her. A murder four years old? It's barely getting any resources. So Maxwell asked if we could track the suspect down."

"You said 'her.' A *woman* did this?" Scrolling through the photos of the murder scene—Yoden's hotel room—I shake my head. "This is too cold and calculatin'."

"You've never met Inara," Dax says, his lips twitching once in what *might* be a smile. "You can't be a sniper without havin' a healthy dose of cold and calculating."

"What's the job? Who am I backin' up this time?"

A single chuckle—so short I almost miss it—and he replies, "No one. You're on your own. Dante Lambert is your contact with the General Intelligence and Security Service in Antwerp. He has reason to believe Yoden's killer is in Boston. The job is to bring her in. Whatever it takes."

The words "you're on your own" play in a loop in my head

until he clears his throat and I set my tablet on the edge of his desk. "Whatever it takes?"

He removes his glasses. It doesn't matter that I'm just a hazy silhouette to his eyes, the power of his stare makes me want to squirm. I'm only a couple of years younger than he is, but right now, I feel like Sister Mary O'Leary is about to rap my knuckles with a ruler. "*Whatever* it takes."

CHAPTER TWO

Zephyr

"Ladies and gentlemen, we're starting our descent. The captain has turned on the fasten seatbelt sign. Please return your seat backs and tray tables to their upright and locked position."

The announcement jolts me awake from the first good sleep I've had in a month. Planes—once I've walked up and down the aisles and assessed every passenger—are the only place I truly feel...safe. Once we're in the air, they become massive safe rooms. No one in or out, no one sneaking up behind me to try to cut my throat, breaking in to kill me in my sleep, or chasing me through a maze of dead-end streets only to shoot me with a tranq gun and bring me back to the cartel.

I shudder, the memories of every single one of those events rushing back now that I'm awake.

The city of Boston spreads out like a glittering jewel in the late afternoon sun, and I wonder if this will be the place I stop running.

As the rows ahead of me gather their belongings, I run a

hand through my newly teal and black-dyed hair. I took a pair of scissors to it before I worked up my latest passport, and I love how light it feels. Alex—the man who saved me and Oliver from the streets and became our surrogate father, until he tried to kill me—would hate it. Kind of the point.

Everything about my appearance is designed to draw attention. Eyebrow ring. Septum piercing. Sparkly blue eye makeup, fake lashes, crimson lipstick. Even the clothes I picked out for this trip are so garishly ugly, no one searching for a woman on the run will give me a second look.

After waiting in the long queue at Customs, all I want is a decent meal—and to wipe all this makeup off my face—but first, I need a place to hole up for the next few days. I've learned my lesson. No more squatting in an abandoned apartment for a full month.

My leg still aches, and I clench my jaw, forcing myself not to limp on the way to the T Station. I have no idea how Oliver found me, but my stupid decision *not* to move around definitely had something to do with it.

Back Bay—one of Boston's ritzier neighborhoods—is a little over thirty minutes from the airport by subway. I had a couple of hours in London before my flight, and I found a handful of recently shuttered businesses in the area that might be suitable for a few nights. Long enough to get my bearings and track down the one person who can help me clear my name.

<hr>

BY THE TIME I feel comfortable stopping for the night, I've walked around Back Bay for three hours. With a bag full of tacos and a couple of bottles of water in my pack, I duck down an alley between two old buildings. A large *"We've moved"* sign covers the front windows of a comic book store, and when I stopped for a cup of strong tea at a local shop, I opened a connection to the dark web and had the blueprints of the entire block in under fifteen minutes.

The front and back doors are both alarmed, but no one ever thinks to secure the rooftop ventilation shafts. Thank God all these turn-of-the-century brownstones have fire escapes. At the far end of the alley, I struggle to move the large dumpster close enough I can jump to the rickety ladder. A loud, metallic screech accompanies the slow turn of the wheels, and I cringe. But it's late enough most of the businesses are closed.

Hauling myself up onto the thick, plastic lid, I test my weight with a couple of gentle bounces on the balls of my feet. Good enough. The ladder's a full foot above my head, but Alex insisted his entire crew keep in shape, and I've done more box jumps than I can count in the past fifteen years.

My hands ache from the impact, but I hang on and scramble rung over rung until I fall onto the first landing. When I reach the roof, my right foot almost slips off the clay tiles, but I changed out of my attention-grabbing attire in a T Station bathroom and put on a pair of black leggings, a dark green flannel shirt, and soft-soled black shoes with killer traction.

At the back of the building, I pry off the air vent cover with my multi-tool and shine a light into the dark space. Perfect. A ten-foot drop, then what should be a short horizontal crawl into the comic shop's back room.

The hardest part of this whole operation? Wedging myself in such a way I can drag the air vent cover back over the opening. Winters in Boston can be brutal, and there's sleet in the forecast tomorrow morning.

Shining my penlight around the top floor, I breathe a sigh of relief. Wood covers the windows. It's mostly empty. A handful of scattered papers, crumpled newspapers and packing material, discarded cardboard boxes.

It's quiet enough I feel comfortable dropping my pack in a corner and continuing down the stairs to explore the rest of what'll hopefully be my temporary home. "Oliver would have a nerdgasm over this place."

As soon as I say his name, I regret it. We were inseparable most of our lives. Knowing he's the reason I can't stay in one place for more than a few weeks makes my heart ache.

Taking my time, I comb through half a dozen boxes until I find a stash of *Wonder Woman* and *Daredevil* comics. A roof over my head *and* interesting reading material? Score. Scanning my light over the rest of the shop, I stifle a squeal. The sign over the back wall reads *Socks Galore* and whoever packed up this place was clearly lazy—or rich—because there have to be two dozen pairs still hanging on pegs. The adjoining wall holds a collection of sweatshirts with various pop culture characters on them. They're dusty, but otherwise brand new.

Snagging a *Doctor Who* hoodie from a hanger, I bring it and a small stack of comics upstairs. Best. Night. Ever.

I chuckle at my bargain basement standards. A bag of cheap tacos, six old comic books, and a clean, soft sweatshirt? This is what my life has become.

Pulling out my little camp light, I turn the dial to the lowest setting, then arrange the rest of my very limited stash. Inflatable camping mattress, sleeping bag, my multi-tool, the new hunting knife I bought just a few hours ago, my laptop, and cell phone.

If this place has power, I'm going to be hard pressed to *ever* want to leave. "Yes!" My fist pump and subsequent dance around the room might be too much, but I don't care. This is more than luck. This is divine intervention. Someone up there loves me.

At 1:00 a.m. on the dot, I navigate to the dark web chat room Dante set up for the two of us. The encrypted wi-fi connection isn't much faster than old school dial-up, but the chat room is text only.

Dante: You safe?

Z: As can be. You?

Dante: We doing the small talk thing? Wasn't sure you knew how.

Z: Shut it. I need to know where in Boston to look for our mutual friend.

Dante: Can't be sure. He's careful. Traced a wire transfer from Rome to the Boston National Bank in the South End two days ago. Spent a little time running facial recognition on traffic cameras in the area, but no matches. Doesn't help that Boston hasn't had a single day without rain in a week.

Z: I can scope out the area. See if any local businesses have cameras.

Dante: Good idea. The name on the bank account is Michael Lawrence. There are twenty-three M Lawrences in the greater Boston area. Got addresses on twelve of them. Sent the data to your secure email.

Z: Eleven of them eluded you? Bullshit. After two decades with AIVD? Doubtful. What aren't you telling me?

The chatroom shuts down without warning, booting me off the server. Either I pissed off the one person who's actually *tried* to keep me alive or someone was about to discover him aiding and abetting a known fugitive. I'll likely never know.

My eyes ache, like my lids are made of pumice, and even my skin hurts. If I have lost him to my frustration, at least I have a place to start in the morning. The Boston National Bank. And a name. Tomorrow is all about recon around the area. If I can find a camera or two that captured Michael Lawrence's face, I have a chance to find him. Then the real work begins.

Convincing him to come back from the dead and help me take the Strauss Cartel down.

CHAPTER THREE

Ronan

TAPPING MY PHONE SCREEN—YET again—I stifle my groan. Ten minutes later than the last time I checked. I've been in this apartment a week and I still can't get used to the quiet.

After my promotion, Trevor and Ford both *suggested* I find a better place to live. Somewhere secure and *not* leased under my real name. I laughed, but the looks they shot me? I got the message. Non-negotiable.

This building has a 24-hour security guard at the front door, cameras on every floor, and biometric locks. It's also twice the size of the postage stamp studio I rented when I came to Boston three years ago. One of the perks of my promotion? A significant raise.

But with the soundproofed walls comes silence. White noise doesn't help. Because underneath that? Still silence.

So I stare at the ceiling. Into near total darkness. I can't get my target—a woman known only as Zephyr—out of my mind. Wren's intel packet on her was only four pages long. Unheard of for Second Sight's tech genius. She can put together a fifty-page file on *anyone*. Hell, when I was guarding Austin Pritchard's girlfriend, Mikayla, she sent me info on Mik's sixty-something boss that included his *high school transcript*. But Zephyr has managed to live her entire life without leaving more than crumbs of info anywhere.

"She's a ghost, Ronan. Best guess? She's between thirty and thirty-five, probably from somewhere in Europe, but heck if I can find out where. I can match her facial features to at least a dozen different passports over the last decade, every one of them with a different name. Whoever she is? She has mad skills."

Mad skills is Wren's highest compliment. If she's stumped, how the hell am *I* supposed to find this Zephyr? The only lead we have? An officer assigned to the murder investigation who told Dax he thinks the woman is in Boston tracking down her next victim. I have a call in to the guy, but he's in Antwerp.

Punching the pillow, I roll onto my side. Something about this case isn't right, but damn if I can figure out what it is.

By 4:00 A.M., I've given up on the idea of sleep. One of the best parts about this building? The twenty-four-hour gym on the first floor. After I pull on a pair of shorts and a t-shirt, I grab my phone and lace up my running shoes. Ten minutes later, *Great Big Sea* pounding out a punishing beat in my ears, I set the treadmill to a fast six miles per hour and start running.

My phone rings, interrupting the band's cover of *It's The End of the World as We Know It*. By the number on the screen, this is the call I've been waiting for. Jumping onto the treadmill's sideboards, I jab the screen. "Ronan Murphy."

"Mr. Murphy, this is Dante Lambert with the General Intelligence and Security Service in Antwerp. You require information about the assassin Zephyr?"

"Anythin' you can tell me, yes. What we've been able to put

together so far isn't much." The gym is empty this early in the morning, and I hope to hell it stays that way. This isn't a conversation I want to have in public.

"She is highly skilled at evasion and stealth. From what we have learned over the past four years, she was a member of the Strauss Cartel for more than a decade. She may have amassed countless kills, but we are only concerned with one."

"Jasper Yoden. I'm aware. Killed in São Paulo four years ago. If you can forward me the case file, it could help me understand her better."

"Of course. We believe she was sent to Boston to kill a former member of the Strauss Cartel, one Martín Levi. He is believed to be hiding under an assumed name. Michael Lawrence. If you find this man, you will eventually find Zephyr."

I press Dante for anything he can tell me about Martín Levi, but all he has is a name and a very old photo. But by the time we hang up, he's sent me everything he has on Zephyr, and I'm one step closer to bringing my target to justice.

Zephyr

Dante wasn't kidding about the rain. Even with a cheap, drugstore rain slicker, I'm soaked to the skin in less than ten minutes. First stop? ReUse and ReSell. Second-hand stores don't bat an eye at cash transactions, and while I have a fresh batch of clean credit cards in my wallet, the more I use them, the faster I'll burn them out.

Rain hat, rain coat, galoshes, and an umbrella. All for under thirty bucks.

If I wanted to, I could steal enough money to manufacture a new identity so airtight, François would never find me. But when I escaped the cartel, I vowed to make up for all the shit I did when I thought we were the good guys.

My side jobs—helping those in trouble—fund my basic needs. Others? Like the flight to Boston? I live in the gray area. My dream? To say I'm a good person and mean it. To go a month without lying to *someone*. Even if only to myself.

Boston National Bank stands tall and proud among all the other turn-of-the-century buildings in the South End. Two dozen different businesses make their home on this block, including a coffee shop. Perfect.

Escaping the rain, I inhale deeply. The scent of pastries is almost stronger than that of coffee, and I might be in heaven. Going out to eat? Not something I can do. Showing my face *anywhere* is a risk. At least for a few hours, I can pretend to be normal. Order a hot tea and a scone, find a table by the window and scan for wi-fi signals from the surrounding businesses I can hack into.

Like that's normal.

"Oh, my God." The strawberry rhubarb scone is still steaming when the barista sets it on a plate and adds a generous scoop of homemade whipped cream to the little bowl on the side. "That smells amazing."

"We make them on site," she says with a weary smile. "Do you take anything in your tea?"

"Milk, please." I pass her a ten-dollar bill and adjust my bright red glasses. They're not prescription and keep slipping down my nose. But tinted eyewear is one of the best ways to confuse facial recognition algorithms. These thick frames obscure the position of my eyebrows, and the polarized lenses, even though they're only a couple shades darker than clear, hide the shape of my eyes well enough.

"I'll have to bring that over to you. Take a seat. It'll be just a minute." The shop is mostly empty—only a single businessman playing on his phone and two moms with babies in strollers along the back wall. No one pays any attention as I take a seat by the front window and set up my laptop.

The first bite of the scone—dipped in whipped cream—tastes like heaven, and I dart a glance around the shop in case anyone heard me moan. I'm off my game. Pretending to be just another local stopping for a bite to eat and a cuppa? This is the most exposed I've been in over a year. The entire time I was in Rotterdam, I only left the apartment for groceries.

Focus. Find cameras you can hack and get the hell out of here.

The barista drops off a tiny pitcher of milk, and I offer her a smile as she rushes off to bus another table. From this vantage point, I can aim my laptop's camera at the front steps of the bank and record everyone who goes in or out. The bell over the coffee shop door jingles, and I hunch down in my seat until I get a good look at the guy. He's young. No older than twenty, and from his accent, he was born here.

He's not a threat, and I blow out a long, slow breath and pick up my tea. No one knows I'm in Boston. When I left Rotterdam, I bought five bus tickets—each with a different credit card—then paid cash for the ticket that took me to Hamburg. If the cartel knows where I am after all that? I deserve to be caught.

By the time I've finished my third cup of tea, the jet lag is catching up to me, despite the caffeine. But I have all the information I need to hack into half a dozen businesses around the bank and see if they save their security camera footage. And an extra strawberry and rhubarb scone in my pocket for dinner.

HOURS LATER, sitting cross-legged on the dusty floor of the comic shop, my hands start to shake. The video I took around the bank this morning doesn't show anyone who resembles Martín Levi. But a tall man with dark hair and cheekbones that could cut through a New York steak appears several times over a three-hour period.

He's careful. Checking out one of the clothing shop windows, hitting up the little cart on the corner for a hot dog, and talking on his phone at the bus stop in the middle of the block. But he's definitely staking out the area. Thank God he didn't decide he needed a cup of coffee.

Boston's a big city. He could be looking for anyone. Hell, he could have been waiting for his girlfriend for all I know.

"Bullshit," I mutter in the semi-darkness. Hints of hazy afternoon light seep through slats of the boarded-up windows. Coincidences in my line of work—my former line of work—get you killed. Or jailed. Or worse.

"We know you stole from us, Zephyr," François says, a glint to his hazel eyes. His lips curve, but that's no smile. More like gleeful anticipation. "Tell me what you took and where you hid it, and I won't have to use these."

The dripping wet paddles hooked up to a car battery fade in and out of focus. I'm so tired, I don't care about the pain anymore. I'd give anything to be able to sleep. Almost anything.

"Go to hell." I spit in his face, and he jams the paddles against the bare skin just above my waist. My entire body jerks uncontrollably, and I swing from the thin ropes binding my wrists, then looped through a chain hanging from the ceiling.

Do I scream? The roar in my ears is so loud, I can't tell. He and his favorite thug, Theo, have been at this for hours. Alternating between the paddles and a belt whipping across my back and legs.

"You'll tell me soon," he says, a singsong quality to his words. "Or I'll start in on that pretty face of yours."

Gasping for air, I paw through my backpack for one of the bottles of water I picked up after leaving the coffee shop. "You're in Boston. Alone. No one else is here, and you're fine." The water is blessedly cool, and after a few minutes, my heart rate slows.

Focus. I need to focus. Figure out who this guy is and why he might have been at the bank today. I *should* be hacking into the clothing store's wi-fi and accessing their security camera footage, but until I know he wasn't after me—or confirm he was —I can't think about anything else.

I'll have to access the Boston DMV to find Martín, and I could probably run this man's photo against their databases as well. But that will take time I don't have. Instead, I access the dark web and pray Dante's around.

After fifteen minutes, I glance down at the clock on the screen. Shit. It's close to 11:00 p.m. in Antwerp. Of course he's not online.

Flopping back onto the inflatable mattress, I stare up at the ceiling. The track lighting runs from one end of the building to the other, and I count the individual bulbs, willing myself to relax. Even if Mr. Cheekbones was at the bank looking for me, he didn't follow me here. I was careful. Doubled back a dozen times, changed clothes in a Dunkin' Donuts bathroom before ordering an extra large tea that was surprisingly good.

But now, I'm exhausted. Dante's not the only one on Antwerp time. Setting the alarm on my phone for three hours, I shut my laptop and roll onto my side. Everything will make more sense after I get some sleep.

If it doesn't, I can always run. Again. Give up my quest to find Martín. I hear Montana is a good place to get lost. Or North Dakota. I don't care where I go, as long as it's somewhere no one can find me.

CHAPTER FOUR

Ronan

After the day I've had, I purposely wait until after five to return to Second Sight's office. I'm not in the mood for conversation. My target was sitting in a coffee shop for three hours today, and I didn't notice until she left.

Zephyr's smart. Knew exactly how to disguise herself so her face wouldn't trigger any of Wren's facial recognition algorithms. Oversized glasses, a scarf wound around her neck and over her mouth... She even walked with a bit of a limp.

Thank God Dax is gone for the day. I do *not* want to explain how I managed to lose her on the fringe of Back Bay. One moment she was two blocks ahead of me, and the next? Gone.

I sprinted to the alley I thought she'd gone down and found nothing but a tall chain-link fence. I'd bet money she climbed it and took off in another direction, but hell if I know where.

Dropping into my chair, I open my laptop and send Wren an email. If anyone can figure out where Zephyr went, it's her. She's offline, and I don't want to call her in case she's resting.

Street View of the area shows me a dozen different ways to

disappear. The T station less than a hundred feet from the fence, a women's clothing store on the corner, and a bus stop across the street.

"Fuck it. She could be anywhere by now." Martín Levi—aka Michael Lawrence—has an account at the Boston National Bank I visited this morning, but despite flashing my PI license and doing my best to charm the manager, I couldn't get an address or phone number for the man.

A burly shadow passes by my open door, and I frown. "Tank? Do you have a minute?"

The former Army Ranger ambles silently into my office and leans against the door jamb. "I'm on the night shift," he says, folding his corded arms across his chest. "Got all the time in the world."

"When you spent that week in Seattle, did Wren and Ripper teach you anythin' about our facial recognition program?"

His full lips curve into a smile. "Wren might have shown me a thing or two."

"Brilliant. Can you teach me how to upload a photo and run it against the local traffic cameras?"

Pulling out my phone, I send the only pictures I took of Zephyr to the server while Tank grabs one of my guest chairs and sets it next to me. Up close, he's almost as intimidating as Ryker. Tattoos cover his arms, the ink only a few shades darker than his skin.

"Crop the photos as much as you can," he says, gesturing to the three images on my screen. "All those background colors will fuck up the algorithm."

I'm shit at this tech stuff, and after two attempts, Tank arches his brows and elbows me out of the way.

"When you finish with this case, you need to go out to Seattle and beg Wren to take pity on you and teach you how to use a damn mouse." With a shake of his head, he crops the three pictures in under a minute, then launches the software.

"Shit. I don't even have a login." *What was Dax thinking when he promoted me? I'm a low-level screw up and always will be.*

"Mum didn't want you," my older brother taunts from the seat of his bicycle. "Why do you think your da' split so fast?"

He and my sister pedal away, leaving me standing on the front steps of the old, run-down row house. At sixteen and seventeen, they can go wherever they want, and no matter how many times I ask to tag along, they always say no.

"Ronan? Pay attention. Ford's keeping an eye on some bigwig senator tonight, and if he calls for backup, I gotta go."

Cracking my knuckles, I relish each pop and use the slight pain to pull me out of my memories. "Sorry. I'm makin' a bags of this case." Tank stares at me like I'm from another planet, and I groan. "It means I'm fuckin' everythin' up. This is my first solo gig. I didn't see the target for *at least* three hours, and then I lost her somewhere between the South End and Back Bay."

"Oh, snap." Leaning back in his chair, Tank blows out a slow breath. "I know I'm the new guy, but Dax isn't one to make mistakes. If he thought you could handle this case, then you gotta trust him."

I wish I could.

Instead of listing the dozens of reasons I think my boss is completely off his rocker, I nod.

Tank's phone buzzes. "It's Ford. Give that at least fifteen minutes before you bail on it. Okay?" He pushes to his feet, and he's out the door before I can answer.

Rather than watch the ungodly slow progress bar, I head for the electric kettle next to the coffee machine and set it to boil. Marjorie keeps a stash of Barry's Gold Blend tea in the cabinet for me, and if I'm lucky, the milk is fresh.

By the time I return with a steaming mug, there are two potential matches listed on screen. The first is a false positive. The woman looks nothing like Zephyr. She's taller, her skin is half a dozen shades darker, and when I play the video, it's obvious her legs are much longer.

The next result loads automatically, and I choke on a sip of tea, the hot liquid burning the inside of my nose. Grabbing for a tissue from my desk drawer, I dry my lips and my keyboard without taking my eyes from the screen.

"There you are, Zephyr." Teal hair falls in an angled bob, and that slight limp is back. Gone is the scarf and bright green rain coat. Now, she's wearing a black turtleneck sweater, a ball cap, and sparkly sunglasses, despite the rain.

The camera loses her as she turns onto Newbury Street, but now, I have somewhere to look.

Zephyr

I'm almost through the Boston DMV firewalls. Another hour, and I'll be able to check every Michael Lawrence in the state. I haven't seen Martín in more than five years, but unless he paid for a hell of a lot of very expensive plastic surgery, I'll recognize him.

The scone is long gone, and all I have left to eat are granola bars, jerky, and fruit leather. Functional, but nowhere near as tasty as my breakfast. If I were here on vacation, I'd walk into a restaurant like a *normal* person and order a bowl of New England clam chowder as big as my head.

I haven't eaten in a restaurant since—

Stop wishing for things you can never have.

Tearing the wrapper on a granola bar, I manage a single bite before my stomach twists into knots. I'm safe here. The cartel doesn't know I'm in the United States.

Then who was the man outside the bank?

While my code runs in the background, I pull up his photo.

Serious, brooding brows. Dark green eyes. A fine layer of stubble. He's built under that leather jacket.

The laptop beeps, and I curse softly. A layer of security I didn't expect. I'll need at least another hour before I can access the DMV database. There's a Dunkin' Donuts three blocks away that's open all night. Locking the laptop so only my fingerprint can access it, I pull a ten-dollar bill from my wallet. An extra-large tea and some fresh air will help me focus, and staring at something other than this dark, empty shop might calm my nerves.

The rain starts halfway back to my hideout. Dammit. I should have brought the drugstore slicker. My wool cap and sweater do nothing to keep me dry.

Turning onto Newbury Street, I freeze. At the far end of the block, the man who was surveilling outside the bank tries the door of the shop next to the comic book store. The to-go cup falls to the sidewalk with a splash, and he whirls around and stares straight at me.

Run. Don't stop. Don't think. Just run.

Footsteps pound behind me, and I hear a rough voice with a distinctly Irish accent call out, "Stop!"

I can't. If I do, I'm dead. The streets in Back Bay are a maze, but after walking for hours yesterday afternoon, I have a vague idea where I'm going. The city is too empty this time of night. The man follows me all the way to Boylston, but thank God, there's a bar full to bursting two doors down.

Getting lost in the crowd shouldn't be difficult. Except I'm soaked to the skin and it's barely forty degrees outside. I can't stop shivering. Drunk patrons shove at me, and I go down, hard, my knees slamming into the concrete.

"Get outta here!" the bouncer growls. His thick fingers wrap around my upper arm, and he jerks me to my feet, propelling me back out the door.

My legs ache with every step, the bullet wound from

Rotterdam still not fully healed. A quick right down another alley and I see my destination up ahead. No footsteps behind me. I can't risk the time it would take to look over my shoulder, but all I need is two minutes to hide. I hope.

The parking garage looks more like an abandoned storage facility than a place for cars. Haphazard stacks of pallets line one of the walls, with disintegrating piles of cardboard boxes in front of a rusty dumpster.

I check the dumpster, but the stench...shit. There's no way I can hide in there. Throwing up will get me caught without question. Instead, I squeeze behind the stacks of pallets. It's a tight fit, but I turn sideways and crouch down on my hands and knees.

Shivers wrack my body, some so strong, I'm terrified they're going to rattle the wood. I'm trapped. And by the beam of light sweeping above my head...I'm about to be caught and lose everything.

CHAPTER FIVE

Zephyr

A BEAD of icy water hits the back of my neck, and I grit my teeth to stop my shiver. Any movement, any reaction, and he'll know where I am. He's close, and whoever he is, he's a pro. My muscles ache. Crammed behind the stack of old pallets, I tense my thighs, desperate to stop the endless pins and needles, then press my hand to my mouth so I don't cry out.

I'm so tired. Tired of running. Tired of nights spent napping in "borrowed" cars, in abandoned buildings, in seedy, cheap motels. But shit. Martín is in Boston somewhere. I feel it in my gut. If I can find him, I can prove my innocence and *maybe* get some semblance of my life back.

A single scuff of his foot gives his position away. Too close. He'll be on me in seconds. It's now or never.

Scrambling to my feet, I take off for the opposite corner of the parking garage, running like my life depends on it—because it does.

"Stop!" The bullet passes so close to my ear I can feel it, and he continues, "Or the next one will be two inches to the left. I don't *want* to kill you, but I will if you run."

Hands in the air, I force my next words out over the lump in my throat. "I'm not who you think I am."

"Really, now? You expect me to believe I'm lookin' at St. Zephyr of the Church of Mistaken Identity? I'm not that daft."

I turn slowly. "Of course not. Because anyone capable of tracking me to Back Bay isn't a complete idiot. But most—if not all—of what you think you know about me is a lie."

His light blue eyes hold mine, and I can tell exactly what he's thinking.

She's full of shit.

"Let me guess? Your job is to bring me in for the murder of Jasper Yoden in São Paulo four years ago." My voice doesn't tremble, but damn, it comes close.

"Congratulations. You're not that daft either." He snorts, the gun never wavering.

I should be searching for a way out. Trying to charm him or surprise him or do *anything* to distract him. But he's not with the cartel. Anyone François sent would shoot me in the kneecaps without a word, then bring me straight back to be tortured for my betrayal.

This man is law enforcement. Or military. His stance, his confidence, his mannerisms all give him away. So I take a risk and try something new. The truth.

"The day Yoden was murdered, I was in Stockholm. Didn't set foot in São Paulo until three days later. January 2nd. It was a Sunday. Ungodly humid, temps in the high 70s. I flew under the name Zara Gomes. Brazilian passport."

"Are those details supposed to mean somethin' to me?" His brows furrow slightly, though he still hasn't moved any other muscle in his obviously toned body.

Dammit, Zephyr. This is not *the time to be noticing your would-be killer's physique.*

With a shake of my head, I force myself to focus on the gun. One twitch of his finger, and it's over. "If you were set up to take the fall for a murder you didn't commit, you'd remember those details too."

He presses his lips together, his stare turning darker—harder even. "Back to me. Down on your knees, hands behind your head. Cross your ankles and interlace your fingers."

Shit.

This isn't a man to take pity on a terrified woman, and I've never been very good at playing the damsel. I don't let my voice break, don't look away, don't project anything but absolute certainty. "If you bring me in—anywhere—I'm dead. The moment I'm processed, the Strauss Cartel will know. They'll find me in hours, and it won't be a single bullet to the back of the head that does me in. It'll be weeks of torture for betraying them, for trying to dismantle their organization. For stealing proof of all their crimes. My death won't be quick or easy, and I'll beg them to end me long before they do."

A single eyebrow twitch is all my impassioned plea garners, and though I won't let him see me break, inside, I'm falling apart.

François told me more than once what he planned to do to me. The three days I spent locked in a basement the first—and only—time he caught me left me with scars that will never heal and memories I'll never outrun.

"Please..."

The man with the gun takes a single step forward, and I know determination when I see it. So I do what he asks. I don't have a choice. Footsteps approach, and his breath warms the back of my neck. Hard plastic bites into my wrists, then he's kneeling to bind my ankles. Panic sends my heart slamming against my ribs. I can't run. Can't even stand up.

Trapped. I'm trapped.

My breath saws in and out of my chest until I bite the inside of my cheek, hard. The pain helps me focus. His warmth recedes, and the absurdity of my current position leaves me confused. What's he going to do? Throw me over his shoulder like a sack of potatoes?

"They're not too tight, are they?"

His question—in that deep voice—shocks me enough I teeter and start to fall, but he catches my arm and helps ease me down onto my ass. Our gazes collide, and is that legitimate *concern* in his eyes? "They're tight, but I'm not in danger of losing any fingers or toes."

Backing away a dozen steps, he leans against the stack of pallets I was hiding behind only minutes ago. Tapping his ear, he says, "Tank? Can you patch me through to the Seattle base? I need them to verify somethin' for me." A few seconds later, he continues, "Base, can you check customs records for São Paulo. Four years ago. Person of interest would have been travelin' under the name Zara Gomes on January 2nd. I need this yesterday if you can swing it."

"Does this mean you believe me?" I ask, carefully stretching my legs out in front of me. The chill from the cement floor seeps into my skin, my wet clothes not doing me any favors, and I clench my teeth to stop them from chattering.

"No. But I've had a bad feelin' about this case since the file landed on my desk. And if you're tellin' the truth and I hand you over? I'd never be able to live with myself."

IT TAKES ten minutes for whoever's in Seattle to get back to him, and we spend every second staring at one another like two alpha wolves in a standoff. The thought almost makes me laugh, except *I'm* the one sitting on damp, frigid concrete with my wrists and ankles bound. *He's* wearing a posh leather jacket and gloves.

Don't ogle your kidnapper. Even if he does have piercing blue eyes. And those dark brows. Rough stubble. Get a grip, Zephyr.

"So what do we do now? Party games? I'm great at Twister."

Mr. Leather Jacket glowers at me. "No."

"Monopoly? Name that tune?" I hate the unknown. And I'm actively shivering now.

"Not interested."

"Got a name?" I ask as I tense one ass cheek, then the other. My entire body is going numb, and if I don't work my muscles, I'll never be able to escape.

"Not one you need to know," he snaps.

After an eye roll, I can't help myself. "So you don't mind if I call you Asshole then? Or Neanderthal?" That earns me a growl, and I keep going. "Irish Death?"

"That's a beer," he mutters.

"I know. I'm thirsty. And cold."

His eyes soften, and he takes a single step forward until whoever's in Seattle must start talking, because he touches his left ear. "Go ahead, base." After a moment, he blows out a breath. "Fuck me. Thanks. Do me a favor? Keep this quiet for now." Another beat, and now he's the one rolling his eyes. "That's *exactly* what I mean. Do I have your word?"

I'm dying to ask what he wants 'kept quiet,' but he's already losing patience with me, and I need to stay conscious if I have any hope of getting out of this alive.

He tucks his gun into a shoulder harness under his jacket and stares down at me. I'm a mess. I've barely slept since I got to Boston, my black pants and wool sweater are soaked, and the cap hiding my hair is askew. Every few seconds, shivers wrack my body, and I almost wish Asshole would gag me so my teeth wouldn't chatter so loudly.

Shrugging out of his leather jacket, he approaches. I tense, ready to fight, but he leans down and drapes it around my shoulders. "My name's Ronan. Ronan Murphy."

"Zephyr. But you knew that."

"I know that's what you go by. You're tellin' me it's your real name?" Ronan pulls out a pocket knife and snaps the zip tie around my ankles.

"Only name I can remember." What the heck is he doing? He's got to know I could do some serious damage if he cuts me loose. Do I fight him? Kick and buck and roll? Or trust that if he cares whether I'm warm, maybe he'll care enough not to send me to my death? In the time it takes me to make a decision, he wraps his hand around my arm and helps me to my feet. "What are we doing here, Ronan?" I ask.

"You're comin' with me." The moment I tense, he holds up his free hand. "I'm not turnin' you in, Zephyr. Not yet, anyway. We're goin' somewhere safe, and you need to tell me why the world thinks you killed Jasper Yoden."

"And you trust me not to kill *you* on the way?" I scoff. "What would your boss think?"

Stop it, Zephyr. You're not doing yourself any favors here.

"He'd kick my arse." Ronan chuckles as he leads me to the far end of the parking garage. A black, compact sedan waits in the shadows, and Ronan tugs me around to the passenger side, opens the door, and guides me down with his free hand on the top of my head so I don't whack my skull on the door frame. My arms are trapped behind me, so he has to secure the seatbelt, then pulls out another zip tie and binds my ankles again. "I'm turnin' on the child locks, so you won't be able to open the door from the inside. If you scream or make trouble, I'll toss you in the trunk. Understand?"

I nod. I shouldn't trust him. Hell, I don't know anything about him, but he exudes honor like some delicious cologne, and when he starts the car, he turns the heat up to maximum. As I start to thaw, I steal glances at him, and I wonder. Is this the day I stop running? Or did I just make the *second* biggest mistake of my life?

CHAPTER SIX

Ronan

NOW THAT ZEPHYR'S teeth have stopped making more noise than a whole troop of step dancers, silence fills the car. When I zip tied her wrists, her nail beds were almost blue, and her skin held all the warmth of a block of ice. I can't trust her, but I won't let a woman suffer needlessly.

"How long were you out in the rain?" I ask, glancing over at her. She stares straight ahead, but her eyes dart from side to side. Trying to figure out where we're going?

"Twenty minutes. I wanted some tea. Walked to the Dunkin' Donuts. Why?" Her wariness bleeds through her tone, and her shoulders hike up.

"Because you were freezin'. Probably hypothermic. Boston winters aren't mild."

Zephyr shoots me a look full of disbelief. "No shit. But you were between me and all my stuff on Newbury Street, asshole. I didn't exactly have time to grab my jacket. Or gloves. Or...anything."

Between her and her stuff? Newbury Street was a wild guess.

"Where were you hidin'?" I ask.

"In the old comics store. When they went out of business, they left a shitton of inventory behind. One of the first times I've holed up anywhere with reading material."

Zephyr sucks in a sharp breath, like she didn't mean to tell me any of that, and when I ask her if she's warmer now, she nods silently and turns to stare out the window. Great. I thought we were making progress.

"Look, I know you have no reason to trust me, but if you want me to let you go—or help you clear your name, you have to talk to me."

"Help me? So far all you've done is tie me up and drive me God knows where. That's not helping me, dipshit. That's kidnapping." With a huff, she sinks deeper into my jacket, and a muscle in her jaw ticks until I approach my building's secure parking garage. Coasting to a stop just before the security camera, I unlatch her seatbelt.

"Crouch down as low as you can. There's a camera over the entrance, and I'm assumin' you don't want your face recorded anywhere."

Shock has her brows arching, but she slides down, curling into a ball on the floor of the car and staring up at me like I've just given her the whole world.

This building is secure as fuck, so getting her upstairs is going to be a challenge. One Zephyr will *not* like.

"You're shitting me," she says when I kneel next to the open passenger door and explain the plan.

"It's either that or you can cram yourself into my duffel bag and I'll carry you upstairs that way." With a shrug, I make a show of my thumb hovering over the key fob. "There's a camera in the elevator and one just outside on every floor."

"Where the fuck did you bring me?" She hunches down in the seat, scanning the parking garage like she expects a *bodach* to pop out any second and put an end to her.

"My place." I shrug. "Safest option. I only moved in a week ago. My boss still thinks I live in Peabody."

"I'm not going to *make out* with you," Zephyr says, shaking her head. "I take back what I said earlier. You *are* an idiot."

"I wasn't suggestin' we lock lips. Only that we make it *look* that way. But it's your choice. I can get the duffel bag." Before I push to my feet, she lunges for me, but with her hands still bound behind her back, she topples over into my arms. "Whoa. Careful, now."

"You're not stuffing me into a bag." Is that a hint of fear in her voice? Her green eyes plead with me, and I reach for my pocket knife instead.

One quick snap and her wrists are free. "I don't trust you not to try somethin', so give me your hands."

"If you pull out another zip tie..."

With a chuckle, I pop open the glove box and retrieve my scarf. "I only brought four with me. This should be a bit more comfortable." Winding it around her wrists, I tie the material tightly, but in a manner I hope will look like she's holding onto the wool. After freeing her ankles, I help her to her feet, carefully angling her so her back is to the camera. "Arms over my head, legs around my waist. Keep your head pressed to my neck like you're kissing me."

Zephyr's lips are soft against my ear. "This is a stupid-ass plan, Ronan. Who's going to believe we're *dating*?"

"No one needs to *believe* anythin'. But we do need to hide your face and get you inside." That shuts her up, and I tip my head back and fake a laugh as I jab the button for the elevator. With how she clings to me, the way her fingers play with my hair, and my arm sliding ever lower toward her ass, we *should* look like we can't keep our hands off one another.

"Is there audio?" she whispers when we're on our way up to the sixth floor.

"No. Another two minutes, and you can stop pretendin'." I

have her pressed to the wall, trying not to notice the softness of her breasts or how her thighs mold to my hips.

Her breath tickles my ear. "Why are you doing this for me?"

I tighten my arm around her, finding the soft skin of her neck with a gentle kiss. "Because for some daft reason, I believe one thing, Zephyr. You're not a killer. I'd bet my life on it."

Zephyr

Clinging to Ronan the whole way from the car, I almost forget I'm his prisoner. That he could turn me in without a second thought and my life would quite literally come to an ugly, agonizing end. But he cared enough to hide my face from the cameras. To make sure I was warm. And he verified customs records from *four years ago* in under ten minutes. Trusting him with all my secrets? I'm not there yet. But he can help me clear my name and maybe...take the Strauss Cartel down for good.

His lock beeps, and I risk a glance. Biometric. A man who values his security. And hopefully...mine?

He sets me down inside the door, lifts my arms over his head, and gently pulls me through the living room, down a hallway, and into a bedroom. *His* bedroom from the dark green duvet, the handful of change in a bowl on the dresser, and the book on the nightstand. It smells like him too. Clean, with a hint of sandalwood.

"Don't move," he says as he opens the closet, fumbling around with one hand until he pulls out another set of plastic flexi-cuffs.

"Only serial killers keep that many pairs of zip ties around, you know."

"Serial killers and private investigators. Do you have to...

uh…use the facilities?" Ronan's eyes never stray from me, and he's positioned himself between me and the door.

"I haven't had anything to eat or drink in six hours other than a single bite of a granola bar. So, no. Why? How long are you planning on tying me up this time?" My toes, which were half frozen an hour ago, are warm again. I could fight him. The gun's still in his holster, and though my hands are bound, they're in front of me. Could I do enough damage to get to the front door? Dammit. I didn't check to see what type of lock was on the *inside*.

"Sit. On the bed. Next to the headboard."

"Why? Is this some BDSM shit? Because if so, we need a safe word. I vote for 'let me go.'"

Ronan cracks a brief smile. "That's more than one word."

"Fine. What about 'beer'? I didn't lie earlier. I *am* thirsty."

With an arched brow, he waits for me to sit, but I'm not about to give in that easily. He reaches for my hands, and I take a step back. "I'll not ask you again."

"No? I don't think you're going to shoot me in your own apartment. Not a great way to lie low." Tugging at the scarf, I try to work my hands free, but the man ties effective knots, I'll give him that.

With a low, frustrated growl, he moves so quickly, I don't have a chance to react before he grabs my wrists and tugs me against him. "You said you left the comic book shop with nothin'. Do you want someone *else* findin' your stuff?"

"I *want* to retrieve my own stuff. If you let me go, you'll never see me again. Tell your boss you couldn't find me. Hell, I'll even help you save face and make it look like I'm in Paris or London." We're close enough his scent winds around me, and I splay my fingers over his broad chest.

"Runnin' won't help you clear your name." His voice softens, as does his gaze. "I'll help you, Zephyr. But I don't trust you yet, and I can't have you disappearin' on me. The man you supposedly killed? My boss knows his brother. This is personal for Dax, and if I don't bring you in, he'll send someone else after you. Someone better than me. Or worse. He'll send *everyone* else after you."

"I don't have much of a choice, do I?" Warning bells should be going off in my head, but it's almost...silent in there as I sink down onto the soft mattress.

Ronan deftly loosens the scarf. "One hand on either side of the headboard post. Please."

The "please" surprises me, and I slide one of my hands around the back of the wrought iron post. The flexi-cuffs tighten, tethering me to Ronan's bed, and he grabs a second pillow from the far side and wedges it behind my back.

"Are you comfortable enough?" he asks, taking a step back. "Do you want a blanket? A beer? Tea?"

"Why do you care?" The moment the words escape, I regret them. He's being *nice*. Solicitous, even. For someone who keeps tying me up.

"Because I'm not a complete arse?"

With a sigh, I swallow the urge to respond with an unhealthy dose of sarcasm. "A cup of tea would be amazing. With milk if you have it. I really wanted that one I dropped before you started chasing me."

He nods, heads out of the room, and busies himself in the kitchen for a few minutes. Once he leaves, I'll be out of these cuffs in no time, but for now, I relax against the fluffy pillows. My arms ache from being bound in various ways for the past hour, but I'm warm and dry. More importantly, François has no idea where I am. For that alone, I'm grateful.

When Ronan returns with a steaming mug and a shot glass of amber liquid, I arch my brows in question.

"If I'd been soaked to the skin most of the night, I'd want a dram of whiskey in my tea."

"Who *are* you?" I ask. "And that's a yes, by the way."

He pours the whiskey into the mug and sets it down within my very limited reach. Drinking will be awkward as hell, but manageable. "This place is virtually soundproof, the door's reinforced, and only *I* can open it. You'll be safe here, and I'll be back in under an hour."

He's gone without another word, and I pick up the tea. Freeing myself should be my number one priority. But instead, I sip what tastes like Irish Gold and wonder why Ronan would even consider taking a chance on me.

CHAPTER SEVEN

Ronan

BOTH THE FRONT and back doors of the abandoned comic book shop are alarmed and appear undisturbed. How the hell did Zephyr get in? Assuming she hasn't vanished by the time I get home, I'll have to ask her.

Leaving her was a stupid idea, but it's not like I could throw her in the trunk of my car while I retrieved her stuff, and sure as shit she's not one to sit quietly in the front seat.

With a piece of foil between the contacts—part of my standard kit—I disable the alarm on the back door and then pick the lock. Shining my flashlight around the bottom floor, I marvel at the sheer amount of inventory left behind. Comics, records, even blind box collectables.

No sign of Zephyr's stuff, though several of the boxes have been rifled through. A set of stairs lead to the second floor, and when I turn the corner, I find everything. An inflatable mattress and sleeping bag, a laptop—lid open, but screen locked—and a backpack. Next to the computer, a half-eaten granola bar.

"I haven't had anything to eat or drink in six hours other than a single bite of a granola bar."

Dammit. I shouldn't care. Except I don't believe she chose this life. Always on the run. Squatting in abandoned buildings. Living off granola bars and jerky.

Someone set her up to take the fall for Yoden's murder, and whoever they are, they're well connected. Given what she's obviously been through over the past four years, I doubt that woman's scared of much, but she's terrified of them finding her.

Carefully, I pack up her stuff, leaving her laptop for last. The fan is running at top speed, so the machine's obviously processing something *big*. From my kit, I withdraw a thin piece of latex film, smooth it over the tip of my finger, and press down on the sensor.

Maybe I'm not completely inept when it comes to tech, because a progress bar fills the screen. My momentary burst of confidence fades almost immediately when I scan the lines of code behind it.

It might as well be written in Klingon for all I can under-stand what she's trying to do. In another window, however, there's a still photo of me from this morning outside Boston National Bank.

Fuck. I should have been more careful. Dax will murder me if he finds out the target was on to me. Then again, she *is* tied up in my apartment.

Dax can't know any of this shit. Not until I have proof Zephyr was framed—proof that doesn't come from her.

The laptop beeps, and the code stops scrolling by. Replaced by the Boston DMV's secure back end database. For a suspected murderer, she's a damn good hacker.

She's also a puzzle. An infuriating, sarcastic, possibly dangerous puzzle. After packing up her computer, I shine the flashlight around the mostly empty space. Erasing all evidence *someone* was here would take me hours, but other than any hair or skin cells Zephyr left behind...the room is clean.

Two steps into the darkness of the first floor, something hard strikes the back of my neck. My hands and knees hit the ground, and a savage kick to my gut makes me retch.

"Where is she?" The voice holds an accent I can't place. Refined. Precise. When I don't answer, another kick knocks me onto my side. Too close to the still healing bullet wound from Edgewater. Fuck. "Where. Is. She?"

"No feckin' clue who you're talkin' about," I manage as I scramble up and reach for my Glock.

The cock of my attacker's gun causes me to freeze, and I risk a glance up at him. The only light comes from small cracks in the wood covering the windows, so all I can see is a dark silhouette. He's taller than me by a couple of inches, and built like a linebacker with a significant beer belly. A glint reflects off the barrel of the gun. His aim is steady, while I'm struggling to find my breath.

"Zephyr belongs to us. I know she was here tonight. Tell me where she went, and maybe, I will let you live."

"Who's askin'?"

Think. This arse is after Zephyr, and if you can't distract him, you're both dead.

"Do you really expect me to tell you?" The man laughs, and I glance around the room, desperate for a way out of this. There! A light switch to my left.

Kicking an empty box in his direction, I spin around, flip the switch, and dive behind a counter. The gunshot reverberates in the abandoned space, and glass shatters.

Shit. A fiery pain burns my shoulder, and a second shot hits the wall behind me. Why didn't I notice the counter was just one big display case?

Because it was dark as fuck, idiot.

Pulling my Glock from the holster, I fire back, but from this angle, hit nothing but ceiling tiles.

"Putain!" the man shouts, his heavy footsteps thudding toward me. My left arm throbs, and a piece of broken glass stabs my palm. I have to get out of here right fucking now.

Rolling onto my side, I take aim and fire two shots. The bullets hit the man square in the chest, and he stumbles back, then crumples to the ground. Staggering to my feet, I skirt the counter, still drawing down on him. He groans and clutches at his torso. No blood. Body armor.

Move.

He's no amateur, and I need to get the hell out of here while he's still down.

As soon as I burst out the back door, I suck in a ragged breath. My shoulder burns, but I don't stop to check how bad it is. Yanking the shard of glass from my hand, I toss it away and start running.

Sirens blare, getting closer by the second. Someone reported the shots. Explaining my presence? Not high on my to-do list, and I push myself harder.

Parking in this neighborhood is impossible, and my car is four blocks away. I hope I'm fast enough to lose the arse before he comes to his senses.

A spitting rain starts to fall, plastering my hair to my forehead. This is the second time I've been shot in less than two months. If I wasn't so certain Zephyr needed me on her side, I'd seriously consider finding a new career.

I DON'T GO STRAIGHT BACK to my apartment. I'm bleeding, and if anyone saw my car in Back Bay, I'll be safer in a clean vehicle. Dax keeps a fleet of black SUVs in Second Sight's parking garage. All registered to a local car dealership whose owner used the company's services when Dax and Ford were the only two on staff. "Feckin' hell. I liked this shirt," I mutter. The wound isn't deep, but it needs stitches. The gash to my hand might be good with only a bandage.

Go upstairs? Or go home? If anyone's in the office, I'm fucked, and so is Zephyr. Entering my code into the key locker, I snag the fob for the closest SUV.

The five-mile drive to my apartment stretches out in endless minutes while I make sure no one's following me, and I pull into the garage, exhausted, pissed off, and in pain.

After I scan my palm to open the door, I stop short. Zephyr sits on my couch, *wearing my bathrobe* while some super hero movie plays on my television.

"What the fuck are you doin'?" I ask, pulling my gun and pointing it right at her head. "I left you tied to my headboard."

She jumps up, focusing on the gun. "Are we back to this again? I didn't leave. I was cold. And filthy. I took a shower, and since I didn't have any of my clothes, I improvised."

"Did you snoop around too? Crack my safe? Are you hidin' one of my guns under that robe?"

Zephyr skirts the couch, her fingers wrapping around the belt. "Want to frisk me? You didn't before, and that was *most definitely* a mistake."

"Keep your feckin' clothes on." I hold up my left hand, then wince at the pain in my shoulder.

"Shit. What happened?" Zephyr rushes over to me, and with a sigh, I holster the gun.

"If I had to guess? Whoever's after you tracked you to that comic shop. Some big arse with messy black hair and a French accent shot me after demandin' I tell him where you were."

Her green eyes widen, and she backs up until she hits the arm of the couch, then sinks down. "Could be one of a handful of guys. But they never travel alone. No matter who it was, it means François knows where I am—or where I was." Her voice

—strong and confident since the moment I shot at her in the garage—falters, and she shakes her head. "I'm sorry, Ronan. If I stay here any longer, I'm putting you in more danger than you'll ever know."

Her steps aren't steady as she heads for my bedroom, and I follow in time to find her scooping up her clothes. "Give me five minutes to get changed, let me have my backpack, and you'll never see me again."

"What'll you do?" Using my body to block the door, I set her pack down behind me. "Because if they found you once, they'll do it again. They were ready to kill me without a second thought. I don't want to think what they'd do to you."

Zephyr stops, frozen in place holding her damp clothing. Her expression doesn't change, determination in the set of her jaw. But her eyes? She's scared. Terrified even.

"You didn't leave. You had the chance. I saw your laptop. Anyone with the skills to hack into the DMV wouldn't let a biometric lock stop them. Stay and let me help you." Dax is going to murder me. Slowly, painfully. But my gut—which I'd stopped trusting after the mess in Edgewater—is telling me Zephyr needs someone on her side.

"Take off your shirt," she says, adjusting the ball of clothes on her hip and gesturing to the bathroom. "And tell me where I can find your first aid kit." When I don't move, she stares me down. "If I'm going to put a target on your back, the least I can do is patch you up first."

Her brief moment of vulnerability fades away. As she passes me, careful not to brush my injured shoulder, our eyes meet, and though this case is turning into a mess of epic proportions, I don't care. Zephyr needs my help, and she's going to get it.

CHAPTER EIGHT

Zephyr

WHY DIDN'T I run when I had the chance?

Because you were warm, and he made you a cup of tea.

This is how screwed up my life is. A man shows me a single moment of kindness, and I turn into an idiot.

Dumping my clothes into a pile on the floor, I lean against the wall while Ronan pulls a first aid kit from a drawer and sets it on the counter. "You don't need to do this."

"Yes, I do. Take your shirt off."

Busying myself setting out gauze, antiseptic, and a suture kit, I pay little attention to Ronan until he clears his throat. "If you don't mind...? You're not the only one who got soaked tonight."

"Shit. Sorry..." I lose my words entirely when I get my first good look at his torso. A Celtic Cross covers the right side of his chest with a beautiful woman—a Siren, if I had to guess—tattooed over his arm and shoulder.

"Are you goin' to patch me up or ogle me all night? If it's the latter, I'd prefer to make a cup of tea first." His smart mouth twitches, and I roll my eyes.

"Hold still." Because I don't trust him—and because I want to—I rest my palm over the Celtic Cross. A light dusting of hair tickles my fingers, and his muscles tense. With my free hand, I pour a generous amount of antiseptic onto one of the gauze pads and press it to the wound.

"Fuck me," he hisses. "That burns." He leans a hip against the counter, and honest-to-God, I didn't expect him to pass out over a little blood.

"No shit, Sherlock. Getting shot usually does. Let me guess. This is your first time." Ronan's skin is warm under my touch, and damn. He still smells good.

"Fourth," he manages through clenched teeth. "Twice in the Army. Once last month."

I meet his gaze, the gauze pressed to the deep gash in his shoulder. "Last *month*?"

Ronan nods to his right side where a fresh, reddish scar mars the skin above his belt. "Through and through."

Running my fingers over the wound, I kick myself when he cringes. "Sorry. I didn't mean—"

"I was lucky. The whole job went sideways at the end," he mutters. "Are you done with the antiseptic already? Feels like it's eatin' through my shoulder."

Shit. Pay attention. You need him, remember?

The stained gauze goes into the trash, and I turn him gently to get a better look at the wound in the light. "Five, maybe six stitches. I can do it, but at the hospital, you'd have anesthetic." Dammit. I don't want to be the cause of more of Ronan's pain, even though going to the hospital is risky in its own right.

"My boss has a doctor on retainer who doesn't ask questions. But he'd sure as shit tell Dax, and then I'd have to explain why I haven't brought you in yet. I can handle the pain." He sets his jaw, staring at the towel rack like it holds the answers to all the secrets of the universe.

"All right, Mr. Broody and Stubborn. Don't say I didn't warn you." Snapping on sterile gloves, I rip open the suture and pick up the needle. With my free hand, I hold the gash closed. As the tip pierces his skin, Ronan stifles a grunt, and his eyes squeeze shut. "Breathe. First one's almost done."

Tying off the stitch as gently as possible, I cut the suture thread and start on the second. By the time I'm done with all five and secure a bandage over the wound, sweat glistens on his brow, and his abs are trembling.

"Ronan? Look at me." I pull off one of the blue gloves and cup his cheek. "You lived. And the stitches are even straight. Let me see your hand now, okay?"

"Gotta sit down." With a groan, he sinks onto the closed toilet lid. Placing his hand over the sink, palm up, he adds, "Don't even *think* about practicin' your sewin' skills again."

"Wimp. With that attitude, I should let you bleed all over your nice new towels." I'm not gentle as I hold his fingers still and pour a healthy dose of antiseptic over the cut.

"Jesus, Mary, and Joseph. Warn a man next time!" Ronan tries to pull away, but I hold fast. "I'm not coddin' you, Zephyr. I've been knocked on the head, kicked, punched, shot, and almost killed in the past two hours."

He's right. I soften my voice and lightly stroke the uninjured part of his palm. "Being an ass? It's my default. You spend enough time on your own and you," I shrug, "forget how to people."

With a sigh, he relaxes. "Get on with it, then. I'll make us some tea when you're done."

"No. When I'm done, you're going to clean up—keeping those stitches dry—and I'll make tea. If the cup you gave me earlier is any indication, we like our tea the same way. Strong, not sweet. A generous splash of milk."

"Don't forget the whiskey." He grimaces as I irrigate the wound. "Check for any small pieces of glass, will you? Please?"

"I am." Turning his hand back and forth under the lights, I'm satisfied. "It's a clean cut. Butterfly bandages and a tight wrap should do it."

"Thank fuck." The words escape on a harsh whisper, and I'm amazed he's still upright.

"Who was it?" Carefully pressing one of the little bandages over the edge of the gash, I fight to keep my voice steady. "Who came after you? What did he look like?"

"Big guy. Six-foot-four, close to three hundred pounds. Mean son-of-a-bitch. He cursed in French but didn't have much of an accent when he was demandin' I tell him where you were."

I swallow hard, then try for one round of slow breaths to calm my racing heart. "Theodore Hallswell. I'm fucked, Ronan. For Theo to find me...? I only trust one person in this world, and if Dante sold me out—"

"Dante?" His head snaps up, and his face no longer carries the weight of his exhaustion and pain. "Dante Lambert?"

The third butterfly bandage falls to the floor. Retreating until my back hits the wall, I tense, ready to run. "How do you know that name?"

Ronan offers me his uninjured hand. "Zephyr. Wait."

"Answer me!" My stomach ties itself into a knot. How far could I get wearing Ronan's bathrobe? A few blocks? It's after 2:00 a.m. The streets should be empty, but that means I'll stand out even more.

"He's my contact at the General Intelligence and Security Service in Antwerp. He sent me photos of the crime scene in São Paulo, a couple of shots of you—none recent—and gave me the name of your next victim."

"I don't *have* a next victim! I've never killed anyone in my life and I'm not going to start now." Focusing on Ronan's hand

—the skin of his palm, the clear lines, strong fingers—I add the last two bandages, then wrap the wound with gauze, followed by a light covering of flexi-tape. "You're good."

Shit. What now? If he's working with Dante, I can't trust him.

Ronan flexes his fingers carefully, only a slight crinkling to his eyes. "You have some skill with field dressin'."

I shrug. "Had to patch myself up a time or two." I take a step closer to the bathroom door, darting a quick glance behind me to where he dropped my backpack. "I'll...uh...make the tea."

With what might be a laugh, he lunges for me and grabs my wrist. "You might be good at hidin' from other people, Zephyr, but I can see right through you. I'd get in the shower, and when I got out, I'd find nothin' but an empty apartment. Until your body washed up on the shores of the Charles River. Or worse. Only a piece of it."

He's not wrong.

"Dante Lambert is the case officer assigned to Jasper Yoden's murder. Or so he says. He asked me to send him regular updates. When I found you on a traffic camera turnin' onto Newbury Street, I put that info into my case notes and sent Lambert a copy. That was before I brought you back here, and like I said...no one knows this address. Not even my boss."

"What about your car registration? DMV records? Hell, there'd be a background check on your record for the lease. *There are ways.*" I don't care how safe he *thinks* we are, he doesn't know François. Doesn't know how far his influence reaches.

I'm shaking now, ready to knee him in the groin and see how far I can get before he catches me until Ronan pulls me closer and wraps his left arm around my waist. "I saw that asshole's face, Zephyr. He's comin' after me now too. We're in this together."

How can I believe him after finding out the only person I trust is working for François? Then again, what choice do I have? If I leave, it's only a matter of time before François tracks me down. And Martín? He'll be dead too.

Staring up into Ronan's blue eyes, I search for a reason to believe him. "How does...together work?" I ask on a whisper.

His fingers cup the back of my neck, threading through my hair, and he dips his head. Not to kiss me, but to touch his forehead to mine. "We trust one another. We're *honest* with one another. About everythin'. Can you do that?"

Warmth seeps into me, and I forgot what it was like to be... touched. To be held. To not be alone. Nodding softly, I relax into his embrace. "I can try."

CHAPTER NINE

Ronan

WHEN I COME out of the bathroom, showered and dressed in
a pair of pajama pants and a t-shirt, I hold my breath until I
see Zephyr standing at the counter. She's clad in a black tank
top and a pair of *my* boxer shorts. As the kettle goes off, she
pours the milk into the mugs, *then* adds the tea bags and hot
water.

"I'm impressed," I say from just outside the kitchen. "Takin'
tea should always start with milk in the cup first."

"Pouring milk into hot tea screws with the taste," she says,
staring between the mugs and the clock on my microwave. "I
didn't know where you kept your whiskey."

"And you didn't snoop? What kind of fugitive are you?"

She flinches, then returns the milk to the fridge. Four hours
ago, I was ready to shoot her if she ran, and now...she's in my
kitchen, looking like she belongs there. "Not a very good one,
apparently," she says under her breath.

Fuck. That was the *wrong* thing to say. Retrieving the
whiskey from the pantry, I uncork the bottle and fill two Glen-

cairn glasses with generous pours. "Thought we could have this on its own while the tea steeps."

"I don't usually drink," she says, her shoulders hunching. "I can't let my guard down."

"You're safe here, Zephyr." After I set the glasses on the coffee table, I offer her my hand. "Come with me."

Her green eyes narrow, but she lays warm fingers over mine and lets me lead her to the front door. With my left hand—big mistake—I rap on the door and stifle my grunt. "Reinforced steel. If anyone stops within a two-foot radius, this display panel will light up and the camera in the peephole will record exactly who they are."

Zephyr relaxes by degrees, though she hasn't said a word.

Pressing my palm to the screen, I wait for it to read my print before a menu pops up. A tiny gasp escapes her lips when I tap *Add Palm Scan*.

"Go ahead. It's a closed system. No internet access. Your prints won't go into any database." I wish I knew how to reassure her, but until I learn what she's gone through, anything I say could cause her to rabbit.

"Why would you...?" she asks, her eyes glistening. "I could disappear."

"Do you want to?" Zephyr's strength amazes me, but underneath the tough exterior, there's a terrified, lonely woman who desperately needs someone to believe her.

"N-no. For the first time in four years...no." She presses her hand to the screen, and the lock scans her palm print. When it's done, the system prompts for a name, and she doesn't hesitate to type *Zephyr*.

"Will you come sit with me?" Nodding toward the couch, I almost stumble as she links her fingers with mine and doesn't let go, even when we sit down and she takes a tentative sip of the whiskey.

"You buy the good stuff."

"For drinkin'? Yeah. There's a bottle of Bushmills in the cabinet for mixin'. I don't partake often. When I do I want to enjoy it." The sweet, spicy drink warms me from the inside out, and after a healthy swallow, I move to the tea. Zephyr brews a good cup, I'll give her that. "Where are you from? You don't have an accent. Not one I recognize."

With a shiver, she cups the tea in both hands, and I stop her before she can answer. "Wait here." My shoulder aches reaching into the hall closet for a thick wool blanket, but the gratitude in her eyes when I return and drape the heavy, hand-made throw over both of our legs is worth it. "Zephyr, you need to tell me if you're cold. Or tired. Or anythin'. You're not alone anymore."

"Do you know how long it's been since I trusted anyone?" she asks. Gone is her biting wit, the sarcastic edge to her voice. Gone too are the walls she's had up since we first laid eyes on one another. "A hell of a lot longer than four years."

"Tell me."

Zephyr lifts the mug to her nose and inhales deeply. "I've always loved the scent of a proper cup of tea."

"My mum insisted tea could fix anythin'."

"Not this." After another sip, she sets the mug on the table and huddles deeper under the blanket. "How much do you know about the Strauss Cartel?"

"Nothin'. There was a note in your file that they were the ones to first recruit you, but that's it."

Zephyr pulls her bare feet up so she can wrap her arms around her knees. "I was fourteen. Living on the streets in Italy with my little brother, Oliver. I don't remember my mama, but Papa had left us two years before. He was sick a lot, but—" she sniffles and presses the back of her hand to her nose for a brief moment, "—one day, he didn't come back to the shelter we were staying in."

"Shit, Zephyr. I'm sorry." I reach for her shoulder, but she shrinks back.

"Don't. We were *fine*. I kept Oliver safe. But one day, I picked the wrong pocket, and a man named Alex Strauss caught me. But instead of turning me in, he bought me hot chocolate." She smiles, like she can still taste it. "Every day for two weeks, he bought me a hot chocolate from this little espresso stand in the piazza. I didn't understand he was grooming me."

Jesus, Mary, and Joseph. Grooming her for what?

I want to ask. I *have* to ask. But how? Thank fuck Zephyr clears her throat and continues.

"He'd seen me steal from half a dozen other people that first day, and eventually, he told me he could use my skills. He had this little 'family.' They were good people. They stole. But only from the rich, and only when they had to. Or when they heard about someone else in need."

"Like fuckin' Robin Hood?" Disbelief roughens my voice, and I stare down at this intelligent, beautiful woman, wondering how she could have believed a line like that. Until it hits me. *She* didn't. A fourteen-year-old girl with a younger brother to take care of did.

Sitting up straighter, she narrows her eyes at me. "Yes. Like fucking Robin Hood. He wasn't lying, either. Not...exactly. For the first time in years, Oliver and I had a roof over our heads. Hot meals. People looking out for us. Alex taught us how to fight, how to pick locks, how to blend in. But he also insisted we read the newspaper, learn history, math, science..." Zephyr sighs, a hint of longing in her green eyes. "He was like a father to us. To all of us. The others weren't much older than I was."

"How long did you stay?" By the affection in her voice, she cared for this man, and I'm even more baffled that he turned on her in such an extreme way.

"Too long." At my raised brows, she continues. "Fifteen years. I'd still be there if Alex's brother, François, hadn't shown up one day and changed everything." Zephyr's stomach rumbles, and her cheeks flush bright red.

Shit. She told you she'd barely eaten. Are you completely incompetent?

"Let me make ya somethin' to eat. I have eggs, frozen waffles, cereal, peanut butter and jelly for sandwiches, and homemade soda bread." I'm in the kitchen before I finish talking, ready to make her anything she wants.

"You...bake?" Her brows shoot up, and she snags her mug and joins me.

"Somethin' wrong with that? I'm not just a pretty face, you know."

The laugh brightens her expression in a way I hadn't expected, easing the exhaustion around her eyes and revealing a smile dangerous enough I could easily lose myself to it.

"What makes you think you're 'pretty'?" she asks.

"Well, my mum always said I was too pretty for football. Of course, I ignored her and played anyway. Not that I was any good at it. Dislocated my knee in the fourth match, and never stepped on the pitch again."

Cutting two generous slices of bread, I offer Zephyr a plate, then set the kettle to boil.

She studies me—the Waterford FC t-shirt, the tattoo peeking out of my right sleeve, the scars on my forearm from an enemy's blade years ago. "You asked where I was from." Long, almost delicate fingers break off a piece of the soda bread, and her lips curve into a sad smile. "Truth is, I don't know. Can't remember my last name. Papa moved us from shelter to shelter for years. He couldn't hold down a job for more than a few months, and we survived on what little he could save until he got fired again. We lived in France, Germany, Spain, Portugal, and Italy. I speak eight languages, and after we joined the Strauss family, Alex made sure we could pass for many different nationalities." Zephyr huffs out a laugh. "I loved Paris the most," she says, her accent so perfect, she could fool the French president himself.

Alarm bells go off in my head every time she talks about what Alex wanted his "family" to do, and she hasn't even begun to tell me the worst of it. I'd pour us both more whiskey in addition to the tea, but I have a feeling I'm going to want all of my faculties until we can clear her name and take these gobshites down.

<hr>

Zephyr

Back on Ronan's couch under the blanket, a fresh mug of tea in my hand and my belly no longer empty, I start to relax. I can't let my guard down completely. Not even with this man who looks at me like he's already decided I'm worth fighting for.

Be careful. Fighting is one thing. Dying is another.

"Don't think I've forgotten where we were," he says, drawing me out of my worried thoughts. "You stayed fifteen years."

I run my fingers over the edge of the blanket, the feel of the rough wool enough to keep me grounded. "Alex used to say we'd never take a job that hurt another person physically. He made us learn how to fight—Aikido, boxing, some Krav Maga, even a little Muay Thai—but only so we could defend ourselves. 'We never throw the first punch.'" After a sip of tea to soothe my dry throat—I haven't talked this much in at least a year—I stare into the mug. "But his brother joined the organization seven years ago, and François...he had an agenda."

A low rumble sounds from across the couch. Did Ronan just...growl? He wears his protectiveness like a second skin, but I haven't scratched the surface of all the hell François put me—and the rest of us—through. How long until he loses his shit completely?

Reaching for the whiskey, he drains the glass and waits for me to continue.

I'm so tired, I want to beg off. This couch is more comfortable than anywhere I've slept in the past six months, and while I won't truly relax—I can't—I could close my eyes and be asleep in seconds.

"He and Alex fought a lot the first few months. But before long, Alex backed down, and François took over. Right before I...*left*, I found out why no one had seen or heard from François before he showed up on Alex's doorstep. He'd been in prison for assault with a deadly weapon, drug trafficking, and manslaughter."

"Fuck me," Ronan mutters. "François Strauss?" He leans over the arm of the couch and pulls a tablet out of his bag. My heart leaps into my throat. If he puts any of this in his case notes or—God forbid, tells his boss—I'm dead.

"Stop!" I snatch the tablet from his hand so quickly, it takes him a few seconds to react. But when he does, his blue eyes darken, and a vein at his temple throbs.

"Zephyr, hand it over," he snaps.

"No. Not unless you swear to me you won't tell *anyone* about me, François, Alex... My life depends on it."

This was a mistake. Trusting him. Letting him in. My own *family* wants to kill me. I might not be related to any of them by blood—other than Oliver—but they're the only family I can remember. And here I am putting my trust in a man I met six hours ago who tied me up, kidnapped me, and...and then took a bullet for me.

Ronan scoots close enough he can drape his arm around my shoulders. I stiffen and try to pull away, but he holds tight. With his other hand, he cups my cheek, and the fresh bandage grazes my chin. "You don't know me, luv, and I don't expect you to trust me. Not completely. But I swear on my mum's life and on the Holy Father himself, I won't do anythin' to put you in danger."

Luv.

It's just an expression. One so very Irish, I don't think he realized he was using it. But it puts a tiny crack in my armor. I should be more concerned. Hell, I should run as far and as fast as I can. Instead, I relax against him and nod. "I believe you," I whisper. "I shouldn't. The last time I believed *anyone*, I almost died. But for reasons I don't understand one bit, I trust you."

CHAPTER TEN

Ronan

ZEPHYR'S SO TIRED, she can't sit up straight, and while I want—no, I need—to know the rest of her story, she's starting to slur her words, and no amount of tea is going to replace quality sleep.

"When was the last time you slept?" I ask, easing the empty mug from her hands.

"Caught an hour here and there today. Managed two straight last night." She yawns, not meeting my gaze.

"Shit, luv. Come on. I need to get my phone charger out of the bedroom, then you can catch some shuteye." Before I can get to my feet, she squares her shoulders and shakes her head.

"No."

The absolute certainty in her tone has frustration prickling over my skin. "No?"

Zephyr shoves the blanket off her legs and sweeps her gaze around the room. "Where's my pack? I need my toothbrush, and then I'll take the couch. I won't kick you out of your bed."

It doesn't take much for me to scoop her into my arms and

carry her where she seems determined not to go. I'm not as built as Dax, Ford, or Trevor, but Zephyr's light enough—even if my injured shoulder does scream at me.

"Put me down, asshole." She shoves at my chest until her palm smacks into the freshly stitched muscle, and I double over as my vision dims. "Shit. *Shit!*" Zephyr tumbles out of my arms, but lands on her hands and knees. Scrambling to her feet, she grabs me around the waist to steady me. "Ronan? God. I'm so sorry."

"Prove...it," I manage. "Take the goddamn bed." Ripples of fiery pain spiral out from the wound, and I stagger over to the bed. Once I have my pillow and phone charger in hand, I turn to find her watching me. "What?" I can't be gentle with her. Not now. "It's a good couch, but I saw where you were sleepin' last night. That piece of shit air mattress was half deflated when I got there. No pillow. No heat. I could see my breath *inside*. Why are you makin' it so hard for me to be a nice guy?"

"Because I'm not going to sleep!" Her fingers clench into fists at her side. Are her eyes glistening? Fuck me. She's close to tears. I don't say another word, and after several long moments, my silence has the desired effect. Her shoulders heave, and she runs a hand through her hair, pulling at the black and teal strands hard enough I'm shocked she doesn't pull them right out. "Four years," she whispers. "I've been looking over my shoulder every single day since Yoden was killed. The only time I *really* sleep? On planes. The moment the fasten seatbelt sign turns off, I walk the whole length of the aircraft, checking out *every single passenger*. If no one gives me the side eye, if I don't recognize anyone from the cartel, then I know I'm safe until landing. *Then* I can sleep. If I'm *anywhere* else, I'm always listening. Always on edge. Always looking over my shoulder. Waking up ten, twenty times a night at every noise, every siren."

"Fuck, Zephyr. That's no way to live."

"Don't you think I know that?" She advances on me, anger

flashing in her eyes. Jerking up the hem of my boxer shorts, she shows me a very recent wound on her left thigh. One that looks a hell of a lot like the one on my shoulder. "This is less than a week old. My fucking *brother* shot me. He's still in the cartel. The boy I took care of, the one I kept safe on the streets, the little kid who idolized me for *years* chose François Strauss over me, and if I'd been thirty seconds slower, I'd be in some small, dark room, hanging from my wrists, and praying for death. One night too long in an abandoned apartment in Rotterdam, and Oliver found me. Probably through Dante—the lying, two-faced bastard. I know this is no way to live. But it's the *only* way I *can* live."

Her chest heaves, but she's not steady, her body swaying with exhaustion and her eyelids fluttering.

I should keep my distance. Hell, I should let her have her way and sleep on the couch. But she's hurting in every way, and dammit. All I want to do is comfort her. To promise her everything will be okay.

Wren—along with the rest of Second Sight—taught me the importance of promises. "You don't say those two words," Wren told me once, "unless you know, without a doubt, that you mean them."

Approaching slowly, my hands loose at my sides, I wait until we're close enough to touch before I speak. "Zephyr, you're not alone anymore. Tell me how I can make you feel safe. I'll do anythin'. You can bag up my phone, tablet, and internet router and toss 'em down the garbage chute. Do you want my gun? It's yours. Want to cuff *me* to the headboard so I can't contact anyone? Done."

She peers up at me, confusion joining the exhaustion in her eyes. "Why would you do any of that for me?"

I shrug, stifling my wince. "Because you deserve to feel safe. Even if it's just for one night."

Zephyr

How did I get here? In a bed with extra pillows, soft sheets, and a down comforter. In a bedroom on the sixth floor of a secured building, with a handsome, protective, and kind man sleeping in the next room. He left his Glock 19 on the nightstand *knowing* I'm wanted for murder.

Before he headed for the living room, he promised me he wouldn't contact Dante or anyone at Second Sight—where he works—without talking to me first. The sincerity in his eyes? I believe him.

I don't know why this man is risking his life for me. Or why I'm letting him. I *should* sneak out while he's sleeping. Run as far and as fast as I can.

But he took a bullet for me. When he removed his shirt earlier, fresh bruises marred his torso, and I know his type. He's hiding all but the very worst of the pain.

Can I actually do this? Close my eyes and fall asleep? Trust that I'll be safe here until the morning? There's only one way to find out.

THE SILENCE CONFUSES ME. So does the mattress. The pillows. It takes me a few moments to realize where I am. In Ronan's apartment. In Ronan's bed. Rolling over, I snag my phone from the nightstand.

Oh, my God. It's...*morning*. Early. Only a little after 7:00 a.m., but I slept a solid four hours. Outside of the flight from London, I haven't done that in...months.

Tip-toeing down the hall, I find Ronan on the couch, small lines of pain bracing his lips. The blanket he used to keep me warm last night bunches around his waist, and in the gray light of morning, the bruises are so much worse. The way his eyes are darting back and forth under his closed lids, he's dreaming —and it's not a good one.

"Ronan?" I drop to one knee and touch his uninjured shoulder. "Wake up." He sits up so quickly, I end up on my ass, my spine hitting the coffee table with an audible *crack*.

"Shit," he says his voice rough from sleep. "Are you all right?" Strong arms wrap around me and he pulls me onto the sofa next to him, gently running his hand up and down my back to check for injuries.

It feels so good to be held, I don't pull away. "I'm fine," I whisper. "I was more worried about you. Nightmare?"

"The *last* time I got shot. Thought I was about to meet Jesus for a bit there." Ronan relaxes, sinking into the cushions, and God help me, I *snuggle* against him. What the hell am I doing *snuggling* with a bounty hunter? One who less than twelve hours ago aimed a gun at my head.

"Tell me about it?" I ask.

What are you doing? Getting to know him? This is a mistake of epic proportions.

He sighs, curling his bare feet under him with a wince. "The company I work for—Second Sight—we're a security and protection firm. Some light P.I. work. Cheating spouses, embezzlement, theft, kidnappin' cases..."

"So bounty hunting is just a side gig?" My attempt at sarcasm earns me a scowl, and he shakes his head.

"This is the first time Dax has taken on a job like this. Jasper Yoden's brother served with him in Afghanistan."

Shit. "So, it's personal for him."

"It is. Which is why I can't—won't—contact him until we have evidence you didn't kill the man."

He's so confident, so very sure in his declaration, that I don't push him—for now. But there isn't proof, and soon, he's going to figure that out. Until then, I'll steal whatever moments of closeness I can. Maybe if I save up enough of them, the rest of my life—however long it lasts—won't feel quite so lonely.

"So, when you got shot...?" My fingers find their way to his side, and I trail them lightly over the fresh scar.

"One of the guys we work with on occasion was high-level Air Force." Pausing to lock eyes with me, he adds, "He was forced out—long story—and went to 'find himself' in Mexico. He found love instead. And orchid poachers."

"Um, *orchid* poachers? Who'd want to steal orchids?"

Ronan laughs, and my heart flutters. Honest-to-God *flutters*. It's never done that before, and shit. I want it to happen again. "Some orchids are worth up to twenty-five thousand dollars."

It's a good thing I'm sitting down. "So the poachers were after him? Your coworker?"

"The woman he fell in love with. She's a botanist at the Smithsonian. When they came back to the States, Austin wanted 24x7 protection for Mik. I was part of that team. The assholes came after her, and they weren't havin' anyone in their way."

I must look worried, because he smiles and tucks a lock of hair behind my ear. "They were armed, but we had a former CIA sniper with us, and he doesn't miss."

The lethality of Ronan's tone silences the fluttering of my heart, sobering me in an instant. "Sniper?"

"Dax is former Special Forces. Trevor's the sniper. Ford was in the Marines. Everyone I work with has military or law enforcement experience."

Shit. If his boss finds out what Ronan's doing—harboring a known fugitive—I'm dead. Hell, we're both dead. My palms start to sweat, and I pull away. "Ronan, this is dangerous. How long until someone comes to check on you? Demands you report in? Hacks into the DMV to find your new address?"

Ronan turns toward me. "This is my first solo assignment.

Up until now, I've been backup to one of the other senior investigators. My guess? Dax is goin' to ask me for an update later today, but he'll leave me be if I tell him I'm workin' an angle. Wren—she's about the best damn hacker in the world—could find me if Dax ordered her to—but he'll give me a hell of a lot of chances to come in on my own first."

"You're not making me feel any better," I say.

"I'll not sugar-coat the truth for you, Zephyr. Which is why I need to know everythin' you can tell me about the Strauss Cartel and why they set you up."

Oh, yeah. That.

I was so exhausted last night, he *carried* me to his bed rather than press me for more details, and there's so much of my life—my story—he doesn't yet know. "I could still run."

"But you won't." Linking our fingers, he squeezes gently. "It's hard, yeah? Bein' alone all the time?"

I haven't cried—truly cried—since I escaped that small, dark basement. Bleeding, broken ribs, electrical burns, scarred inside and out in ways that will never fully heal. But in this moment? I'm close. He's right. I'm so fucking lonely. Having to do *everything* on my own. Watch my back every step. Hide who I really am from *everyone*.

"Zephyr, I know provin' your innocence won't be easy. Or without risk. But I brought you back here because I looked into your eyes and I saw how much you needed *someone* to believe you."

A single tear fights to escape, but I blink hard, forcing it back where it came from. If Ronan gets hurt, that'll be the end of me. Maybe not my life—though that's possible—but of something just as precious.

Hope.

CHAPTER ELEVEN

Ronan

After breakfast, which Zephyr attacks like she hasn't eaten in months, we sit next to one another on the couch with her laptop in front of us. "Dante will expect me to check in."

The venom in her voice tells me she'd rather string the arse up by his toes and torture him. Slowly and painfully. Before this whole mess is over, he'll regret the day he was born. Snagging my phone from the side table, I groan. "He's messaged me three times since last night."

Zephyr snorts. "Probably hoping you bled out in a ditch somewhere after Theo shot you." Her eyes widen, and her entire body tenses. "Please tell me your phone isn't trackable."

"What do you take me for? I told you last night I wasn't that daft. What about your laptop?" If she wants to doubt me, she'll have to defend her own tech as well.

She answers with an eye roll, then seems to think better of the action. "Sorry. This is all new to me. Trusting that someone *else* knows what they're doing."

I nudge her thigh with mine. "We'll work on it, luv."

Fuck me. Where the hell did that come from? We're not even friends, let alone...more. But she's wearing my clothes, smells like my soap, and she's barefoot, quite obviously *not* wearing a bra, and the longer I spend close to her, the more I wonder what it'd be like to kiss her.

Her cheeks flush bright red, and she boots up her laptop. "I'm sure Theo reported in. So Dante knows I wasn't at the comic shop when you got there. Did he see you pack up my stuff?"

"He was waitin' downstairs when I finished. Can't be sure he hadn't been upstairs before I got there, but I picked the lock on the back door after I disabled the alarm system. I'd lay odds he arrived after I did."

Zephyr doesn't share my confidence, turning and holding my gaze. "Would you bet my life on it?"

"Fuck me. No." Shame prickles along the back of my neck, and I want to tell her I'll keep her safe, but the only promise I can make? That I'll stay by her side until the end.

Flopping back against the cushions, she closes her eyes, her lips pursed, and a little furrow in the center of her brow. Her breathing takes on a rhythmic cadence. A deep inhale, a long hold, and an even longer exhale. Slowing down her heart rate, calming her mind. I know the technique. Both Ry and Dax used it when they served, and it's how we start our monthly staff meetings.

"Ronan?" she says after a full three minutes. Her eyelids flutter open, and from her tone, she still expects me to change my mind and turn her in. "I know you don't have any reason to trust me, but..."

Cupping the back of her neck, I lean in so close, her warmth seeps into me. "We're not doin' this again, luv. I trust you."

"Why?"

The pain in that single word sends me over the edge, and I

seal my lips to hers. She tastes of tea, of maple syrup, of promise. And I don't want to let her go.

"Stop. Please," she whispers. Her hands tangle in my hair, and though she breaks off the kiss, she doesn't pull away. "I've lost everyone I've ever cared for. I can't—I *won't*—let myself believe it'll be different this time."

I'm going to find the people who stole Zephyr's hope and turn them to dust. Holding on, I close my eyes, memorizing her scent, the feel of her, the heartbreak in her voice. "Believe for *this* moment. This *one* moment. Can you do that?"

"I don't know."

Shifting so I can cup her cheek, I draw my thumb gently under her left eye. A single tear balances on her lower lid. "Well, I do. Get on with it. Whatever you were goin' to do. I trust you're not about to throw me to the wolves."

Zephyr draws in a shaky breath, then turns her full focus to her laptop. I'm not prepared for the loss of her closeness, her warmth, the connection we shared. But we're on borrowed time, and clearing her name is a hell of a lot more important than kissing her again, even if it's the *only* thing I want to do.

I don't understand half of what's happening on screen. Wren would probably squeal and claim Zephyr as her new best friend if she were here. After a minute or two, she launches a chat program.

Z: You there?

Her fingers drum against the machine's black case over and over again until the cursor on screen stops blinking and another line of text appears.

Dante: Was worried. It is not like you to be late checking in.

Z: Someone jacked all my shit. Had to find a clean laptop and phone.

Dante: Random theft? Or were you made?

Z: Don't know. Playing it safe either way. Not staying anywhere more than a few hours. Our mutual friend never showed at the bank yesterday. Can you flag his account? Do anything that would require him to make an in-person visit?

Dante: I'll see what I can do. Stay safe.

The chat window vanishes, and Zephyr runs a hand through her hair, highlighting the blue and teal streaks. "This could be suicide. But Dante will send Theo—or whoever else is in Boston—to stake out the bank now that I more or less confirmed I'm going back there. Last night, I hacked into three shops on the same block, so I have full access to their security camera feeds. If we keep an eye on all of them, maybe we can figure out how many people François sent after me this time."

"You really don't think he'll suspect you're onto him?"

She offers me a weak smile. "Not if you can convince your boss you're close to catching me."

Leaving Zephyr at my apartment alone doesn't sit well with me. I'm not worried about her running. I'm terrified that I haven't been careful enough. That Dante Lambert has the resources—and the motivation—to find out where I live.

Ronan Murphy didn't sign my lease. Patrick O'Roarke did. Patrick has a driver's license, passport, credit cards, and enough to his backstory no one will ever suspect he's a figment of my imagination. Not even Wren knows his name. Dax has three separate resources the members of Second Sight can use for fake IDs, and when I joined, he handed me their names.

"Every one of us has at least five separate identities we can use if we're ever burned. Marjorie will set you up with a fifty-thousand dollar off-shore account you can use to pay for the work. Don't tell me the names you picked or who you used to set everythin' up. Safer for everyone that way."

If Dax wanted to, he could probably track me down. But he won't. Not unless I give him a damn good reason to.

Parking the SUV back in the garage, I return the key to the lock box. I'll pick a different vehicle to drive home and call the cleaners to take care of the blood staining the seat of my sedan.

"Morning, Marjorie," I call as I head for my office.

She runs after me, and when I stop and turn, lowers her voice. "Dax wants to see you, and he's in a mood."

Brilliant.

I don't pause at my office. Don't set my bag down or make tea. No one would *ever* accuse Dax of having a sunny disposition, but for Marjorie to warn me about his current mental state, it must be bad.

Four quick raps on his office door—we each have our own unique knock so he doesn't have to wonder who wants to talk to him—and he snaps, "Get your ass in here, Ronan."

Fuck. It's worse than I thought. A few locks of his hair stand up, like he's been tugging on them—a sure sign he's frustrated or angry—and the moment I shut the door behind me, he gets to his feet.

"What the fuck were you thinkin'? I've spent the past few hours on the phone with Boston PD, tryin' to convince them it was a goddamned coincidence *your* car was spotted less than two blocks away from an abandoned building on Newbury Street where at least six shots were fired last night."

"I got a lead on Zephyr. Facial recognition match on traffic cameras in the area."

Dax feels around for the arm of his chair and carefully sits back down. "And?" Steepling his fingers in front of him, he waits for me to continue.

"The only buildin' showin' signs of entry was the old comic book shop. I checked it out and found a backpack with a change of clothes, a sleepin' bag, and some granola bars inside. No Zephyr."

"Then how'd you get yourself shot?"

At my sputtering, he shakes his head with a sigh. "Ford

checked out your vehicle as soon as I got off the phone with Detective Barton. Your steering wheel and front seat were covered with dried blood."

"Were?" I ask.

"The cleaners left an hour ago. Barton's a good cop, and it wouldn't surprise me if he showed up with a warrant before the end of the day."

"Fuck me. Dax, I'm sorry. I didn't think—"

"No, you didn't. We're a team here, Ronan. A family. We don't keep secrets, and we sure as *fuck* don't go dark when we get in trouble." Rubbing the back of his neck, he spins his chair around to face the window. Though the temperature isn't much above freezing today, the sun's out, and this time of morning, it streams into Dax's office. He might not be able to see more than shadows and vague hints of color, but he told me once he can feel the warmth of the sun through the glass.

"When I came down the stairs with the backpack, a man attacked me from behind. Hit me over the head, landed a couple of good kicks. Then demanded I tell him where Zephyr was. We fought, and he shot first. Hit me in the shoulder. The whole encounter only lasted six, seven minutes. I fired four rounds. Two hit him square in the chest, but he was wearin' body armor. I verified he was still alive, then got the fuck out of there."

Dax braces both hands on the window, and his shoulders relax slightly. "Still doesn't explain why you didn't call me as soon as you were safe. Or why you didn't check your fucking messages or show up here until after 10:00 a.m."

Pulling out my phone, I swear under my breath. Five texts since I left my apartment an hour ago. "These all came in while I was drivin'. Figured you wanted an update on the case, and that's what I was comin' here to do."

"Well, go on, then. Finish your report." He doesn't turn around, his fingers splayed over the glass like he needs the warmth to keep him from knocking me on my arse. Knowing Dax, he probably does.

"Are you *certain* Zephyr is the one who killed Yoden?" I ask. I have to force my next words out over the fear that this will be the last case I ever work alone. "The asshole with the CZ75 wasn't interested in bringin' her to justice. He wanted her dead."

Dax sits up straighter, his chair completely silent as he spins to face me. "You read the same file I did. Zephyr's prints and DNA were all over the crime scene. Yoden had corresponded with a friend in Brazilian Intelligence three times over the week prior. He knew he was being followed, and his last email contained a photo of a woman that matches Zephyr's description."

"Somethin' about this case doesn't feel right." Mostly convinced he's not about to beat the crap out of me, I sink into the chair across from him. "If she's an assassin, why the blood and prints at the scene? By all accounts, she's between thirty and thirty-five years old. Wren found less than a dozen photos of her, yet Yoden managed to take one? The evidence in that file is textbook. And the very first rule you taught me?"

"If things appear too perfect, they probably are." Dax takes off his glasses and rubs his eyes. "I remember. But that doesn't change the assignment. She's wanted in half a dozen countries for various crimes, and I told Yoden's brother she'd be brought to justice."

For years, I could never get a read on Dax. His personality was that of an angry boulder, and I was convinced the man didn't feel a fucking thing. Now? I don't know if it's his wife, Evianna, who softened him around the edges or his brother-in-arms, Ryker McCabe, walking back into his life that did it. Maybe both. But he's hurting, and I don't know why.

"Dax? Is everythin' all right?"

For a long moment, he doesn't respond, and I don't know if

I should ask him again or ignore the silence growing between us. Leaning forward, I'm about to tell him it's none of my business when he swallows hard and slides his glasses back into place.

"Maxwell's wife called me last night. Max had a heart attack at his gym. By the time the EMTs showed up, he was gone. I made him a promise, Ronan. Justice for his brother. And you know how we all feel about promises."

"If you make a promise, you keep it." Wren's words echo on a loop, and I wonder if Dax is hearing them too. "I know."

"Find Zephyr and turn her over to the authorities. I'll make some calls and delay extradition back to Antwerp until Wren can do some more digging into the crime scene reports and any aspect of Zephyr's file you think is 'too perfect.'"

"After what happened last night, I don't think that's a good idea."

Dax's brows shoot up. "Excuse me?"

"If Zephyr ends up in custody, I think whoever shot me will go after her. We can't turn her in, Dax. We'd be signing her death warrant."

CHAPTER TWELVE

Ronan

Before I leave Second Sight, I code myself into the equipment room. Dax knows his shit. When I was protecting Austin and Mik in Edgewater, Austin told me Dax, Ry, and Ripper had the best instincts of anyone he'd ever met.

If I hadn't fucked up last night, maybe he would have been in more of a mood to listen. I heard the sirens. I knew the police were on their way, and I didn't report in.

"If you ever get in trouble, call me or Ford. I don't care what it is. Day or night. We protect our own. No matter what."

My very first day on the job, Dax and Ford drilled that order into me over and over. Handed me an untraceable phone with both of their numbers saved. And I didn't even send him a text to let him know I was all right. I'm surprised he didn't forbid me from ever using the company SUVs again.

In the equipment room, I go through the meticulously labeled drawers until I find a pair of bone-conduction ear pieces, a signal jammer, and a GPS kit with four of the dime-size tracking units with built-in panic buttons. Signing each piece of tech out with my initials, I tuck them all into my bag.

The GPS kit and signal jammer, I can explain away. But the earwigs? That's not going to be easy. I hope to all that's holy in this world no one decides to do inventory this week.

On my way back down the hall, Trevor stops me. "Dax rip you a new one yet?"

"I won't be sittin' down for a few days. Does everyone know?"

Trevor chuckles. "If they were in the office, they know. Dax wasn't exactly *quiet* when he told Ford he was going to kick your ass six ways from Sunday."

"Brilliant. My first case is goin' to get me demoted." Slinging my bag over my shoulder, I wince.

You got shot, eejit. Be careful.

"You okay?" Trevor narrows his eyes at me, then takes a step back. "Shit, Ronan. What happened last night?"

I can't ignore the man. Back in January, I flew down to Venezuela with Dani—his fiancée—met Ryker, Graham, and Austin, and broke Trev out of the most notorious prison in the world. *La Cripta*'s Sublevel 5 had a dozen cells, none big enough for the prisoners to even sit up in. The warden, General Ochoa, kept the temperature near freezing, the lights bright enough the prisoners were never allowed to sleep, and tortured them whenever he felt like it. Trevor spent three days in one of those cells and barely survived.

"I'm not goin' to be worth shit unless I get some caffeine." Gesturing down the hall toward the small kitchenette, I wait for Trevor to nod.

"We can take this to the roof, if you'd prefer."

"Yeah. That'd be good." Ford, Clive, Ella, Vasquez, Marjorie...they don't need to hear how bad I fucked up. The rooftop garden is heated, secured, and above all, peaceful.

Ten minutes later, we step out of the elevator, steaming

mugs in hand. Easing myself down onto one of the benches with a groan, I let my gaze wander to the citrus trees heavy with fruit. The heaters keep the garden at the perfect temperature, and Dax brings oranges to Evianna once a week.

"So, spill it," Trevor says, stretching his legs out in front of him and crossing his ankles.

I tell him everything—except how I captured Zephyr, brought her to my apartment, and agreed to help her. Trevor's family, but I have no doubt he'd pick Dax over me every time.

"I can make some calls. See what the CIA knows about Yoden's murder." He drains the last of his coffee and sets the mug next to him. He pushed the cuffs of his sleeves up a few minutes ago, and thin scars encircle his wrists from so long in handcuffs. "You have good instincts, Ronan. It's why Dax sent you on the job for Austin. Why he promoted you."

"I think he's regrettin' that decision at the moment."

Trevor shoots me a look that tells me to shut my trap and listen. "He's not regretting a thing. Except not drilling it into your thick Irish skull that we're a family here. That we don't try to 'handle shit' on our own when there's an entire team of people—here and in Seattle—ready to help, no questions asked."

The urge to tell Trevor the whole truth is almost over-whelming, but I can't break the fragile trust Zephyr put in me. "She's innocent, Trev. I'd bet my life on it. She didn't kill Yoden, and there's more to this case than Dax wants to admit."

He studies me for so long, I fight the urge to squirm. The man is unnerving. Almost as bad as West—the former Navy SEAL and tactical expert working with Ryker in Seattle. I never asked him much about his past, but on the rescue mission to Venezuela, learned his best friend—and Dani's brother—committed treason, kidnapped Austin, tortured him, and was going to kill him. Until the CIA sent Trevor to put an end to Gil first. But Ford told me Trevor has over a hundred kills on his ledger. That much blood? You can't make up for that. Even if they were sanctioned by the United States government.

"Choose your next words carefully," he says, his voice low and deadly serious. "How can you be so sure?"

Fuck. He knows. Or at least suspects. "I almost caught Zephyr on Newbury Street. Got within a hundred yards of her."

"Care to explain 'almost'?" Trevor asks.

Evade, redirect, ignore. With his CIA training, he'll spot a lie. Technically...I *did* get close to her on Newbury Street. Hopefully that kernel of truth will keep me out of Dax's crosshairs.

"She told me she wasn't in São Paulo on the day of the murder. Flew in three days *later*. For fuck's sake, she gave me the name on the passport she was using and Wren verified it." I'm perilously close to crossing every line in the book—with Trevor, with Dax, and with Zephyr—but I'd bet my life she's innocent, and I need *someone* to believe me.

"Any assassin in the game for more than a couple of kills knows how to fake customs records," he says. "What else you got?"

"My gut." I shrug, pulling on the stitches in my shoulder and wincing. "The evidence doesn't add up. If she's this master assassin, why leave prints and DNA behind?"

With a frown, Trevor stares at the orange trees, his eyes unfocused for a moment, before checking his watch. "I have a conference call in twenty minutes. Foster kid a week away from adoption and his drug-addict birth father kidnaps him."

"Shit. Is the kid in danger?"

His shoulders tense up, and I regret asking. Trevor spent most of his childhood in the system, and from what little he's shared with me, his memories of that time aren't good. "The biggest danger is that the father will disappear with the boy. From all reports, he loves the kid. He's just not stable enough to be a parent." Pushing to his feet, he snags his coffee mug and pins me with his stare. "Give me access to the case file and I'll make some calls. If I find anything, I'll let you know."

He's through the stairwell door before I can thank him. I'm too sore for anything but the elevator, and I only stop in the office long enough to pick up my bag and put my empty mug in the dishwasher. I need to get back to Zephyr before my nerves fray any further. And send a message to Lambert to see if I can catch him in a lie.

"ZEPHYR?" My living room is empty. Her laptop sits on my coffee table, locked and still running, but her backpack is gone. I knew I shouldn't have left her alone. Poking out from under the computer is a folded piece of paper, and I grab it. I don't care what her excuse is, but I have to know.

Ronan,

I'm going to the South End. Saw at least two members of the cartel trying to be unobtrusive, and I can't let them get to Martín if he shows up at the bank. I'll be back by six. Don't touch my laptop.

Zephyr

"Goddammit!" Crumpling the note in my fist, I throw it across the room. She couldn't wait a couple of hours for me? Or send me a text message? I gave her a brand new burner phone before I left and programmed my number into it. I can't let her risk herself in the open alone. Not when at least two people who want her dead—or worse—are out there.

The locked trunk in the bottom of my closet—another investment Ford and Trevor recommended—contains my standard go bag along with everything I need for in-person surveillance. A tweed flat cap to hide my hair, dark glasses, a large overcoat with padding in the shoulders to disguise my build, gloves, and a thick scarf. The small gun safe behind a false panel in my nightstand requires my thumbprint, and I clip the holstered Glock 19 to my belt. A smaller, backup piece straps to my ankle under my black jeans.

If I find her—alive and free—we're going to have a serious discussion about trust. And how a lack of it could get both of us killed.

TRAFFIC anywhere in Boston is maddening, which is why I usually take the T. But evading pursuit on the subway? Not as easy as movies and TV make it look. By the time I find a spot to park, it's almost 2:00 p.m. and according to the palm scan on my front door, she's been gone for three hours.

My last attempt at surveillance failed miserably if the video Zephyr captured of me is anything to go by, so I keep my distance, stopping at a news stand to buy a copy of the Globe and making small talk with the owner, all the while scanning the area for anyone who looks out of place.

A flash of red catches my eye, and I stare as a large crowd quite obviously on a walking tour of the area passes across the street. *There.* In the center of the group, a woman in a flashy red leather jacket, tight jeans, and platinum blond hair appears to be nodding along at something the tour guide is saying, but her gaze is fixed on a man leaning against the wall of the bus stop.

I'll give her props for her disguise, but if I can recognize her, so can someone else.

Saying my goodbyes to the news stand owner, I tuck the paper under my arm and cross the street. Fuck me. The man at the bus stop has Zephyr's eyes. Her chin. If that's not her brother, Oliver, I'll *eat* this hat. In under a minute, she'll pass right by him. What the hell is she thinking?

I don't have time to stop her. The best I can do is create a diversion. "Taxi!" I shout, doing my best to hide all evidence of my accent. Stepping out into traffic, I raise my arm like I'm trying to hail a cab, even though I haven't seen one the entire time I've been here.

Two cars lay on their horns, and at least one person rolls down his window to call me an asshole, but it does the trick. Oliver turns in my direction, and Zephyr drops to one knee to tie her shoe less than a foot away from him.

Anger and panic churn in my gut. She's going to get herself killed. Oliver pulls out his phone and starts texting. As soon as Zephyr finishes with her shoelace, she pops up and darts around the crowd and away from her brother. Thank fuck. I cut through an alley on the way back to my car, and when I exit onto a side street, I almost collide with another pedestrian.

"Sorry, mate," I mutter. I'm about to look up when I notice his hand. A tattoo of a snake crosses his knuckles. I've seen it before. When I checked to make sure the asshole at the comic shop was still breathing. Theo.

He elbows me out of the way with a snarled, "Watch where you're going, shithead," and rushes down the street toward the bank.

If it had been any brighter last night, if I'd foregone the heavy coat and hat, he would have made me. My heart pounds half out of my chest until I'm back at the car. I have no idea where Zephyr went and I'm sure as fuck not going to text her. Any distraction could get her killed. So I do the only thing I can. Go back home and offer up some prayers that she'll soon join me.

CHAPTER THIRTEEN

Zephyr

I CAN'T BELIEVE that worked. Oliver didn't recognize me, and I had just enough time to clone his mobile before the tour group took off again.

Now that I can see everything on his device—including any text messages he sends and receives—I crouch down behind a dumpster in an alley, as he texts François, Alex, and Theo.

Oliver: The bank closes in an hour and no sign of Martín or Zephyr. Are we certain Dante's still loyal?

François: He knows what will happen to him if he is not. Your sister is a smart woman. We will study the video you took when you return. She may have been in disguise.

Oliver: I know my own sister. She's not that good at disguises.

Clapping my hand over my mouth to stifle my snort, I tuck the phone into my back pocket. Oliver wouldn't know a good disguise if it hit him over the head with a sledgehammer.

I can't leave the area until 5:00 p.m. If Dante did flag Martín's account and he shows? I'd never forgive myself. But my phone gives me access to a security camera feed with a clear view of the bank's front entrance, so I ease myself down to the ground, pull my knees in to my chest to conserve as much body heat as I can, and wait.

———

THE LOADED PIZZA in the box balanced on my hip smells amazing. I hope my peace offering smooths things over with Ronan. I know he won't be happy I went off on my own, but as soon as I saw Oliver and Theo on the security feed, I *had* to make sure Martín didn't walk right into a trap *I* inadvertently set for him.

Placing my palm over the scanner, I'm almost surprised when the locks disengage. Most of the apartment lights are off. Ronan sits on the couch, a glass of whiskey in his hand and the bottle on the table in front of him next to my laptop. The laptop he unlocked. The laptop with a dark web facial recognition program on screen.

"Um. Hi."

"Lock the door, will you?" The lack of emotion in his voice sends goosebumps racing down my arms. The sound of the deadbolt is so loud, I almost flinch.

"I brought pizza. And information," I offer. Sliding the box onto the counter, I stop a few feet from the couch.

"You *left*." Ronan slams the glass down on the table and stalks over to me. He's a good six inches taller than I am, and I have to crane my neck to meet his gaze. "I gave you my trust, and you left. You're not on your own anymore, Zephyr. I thought we'd agreed on that."

"No." Anger has me drawing up to my full height, hands on my hips. "*You* agreed and I told you I'd try. That I wasn't good at trusting people. And I *did* trust you. I told you where I was going and left all my stuff here. Well...most of my stuff."

"That's not the point. You risked your life—alone—for no good reason. If you'd called me, I would have met you there.

Instead, I had to track you down, watch as you get within a foot of your brother—the brother who tried to *kill you*—and then run right into the arse who shot me!"

"What? Theo? You saw Theo? Are you okay?" I grab his hands, but he jerks away. "Ronan, talk to me!"

"That's rich. *Now* you want to talk?" He shakes his head. "Theo didn't recognize me. Neither did you, apparently. And you're tryin' to change the subject. We're still talkin' about you not trustin' me."

"How many times do I need to repeat myself? I trust you. But *you* need to trust that I've been on my own, on the run, for longer than you've been working for Second Sight. I know a thing or two about keeping myself safe. And you stopped being my keeper when you stopped tying me up."

I'm done with this conversation, and after more than an hour in a dirty, freezing alley, I need a shower. Turning on my heel, I head for the bathroom and slam the door.

The first thing I discovered about Ronan last night after I sawed through the flexi-cuffs? He has a bathroom to die for. Rainfall shower head with multiple steam jets, heated floors, and towels so thick, they could double as pillows. Shedding the bright red leather jacket, black wool turtleneck, and jeans, I'm about to unhook my bra when the door bangs open. I flinch, but don't bother grabbing a towel. He's already seen everything.

"Fuck me," Ronan says quietly. "Your back..." His warm fingers trace one of the thicker scars. I remember that one. Theo took a serrated blade to my shoulder. Then poured vodka over the wound.

"Can't let that get infected," François taunts from the corner of the room. "You are going to suffer more than you imagined possible before I kill you, little street rat."

"Zephyr?" Ronan wraps his arm around my waist from behind, and I relax against him. "What happened?"

"Six months after Yoden was killed, I got sloppy," I whisper. "Oliver, Theo, and Robbie ambushed me coming out of a hostel in Germany. I woke up in a basement, hanging from my wrists. They had me for three days. I'm only alive because my brother's girlfriend slipped me the key to the handcuffs when she brought me some water. And François killed her for it."

We don't speak for several long moments, and I want to tell him everything. How the fear of capture was nothing compared to the terror I felt in that basement. How last night was the first night I'd spent in a proper bed in months. How I've ached to be held for so long, I can't force myself to pull away.

His lips skim my ear, and something deep inside me cracks into a million little pieces. Curling inward, I try to put myself back together, but it's no use. With one feather light kiss, he broke me.

"Don't hide from me, luv," he whispers. "I won't deny I want you. You're beautiful. But it's more than that. You don't back down from a fight. You stand up for yourself, for what's right. And you're brave as fuck. But I'm terrified I'll wake up tomorrow morning to find you gone, and I'll never see you again."

"I won't leave." Turning in his embrace, I risk gazing into his deep blue eyes. I could get lost in them. In his arms. His kiss. "I don't know what happens next, Ronan. With us, with the cartel...with any of it. But I want to find out."

He cups my cheek, a fresh bandage wound around his palm. "I'm sorry I lost my temper. I should have trusted you. Can you forgive me?"

I nod, the words trapped in my throat. Thank God, Ronan understands what I need.

"I'll leave you to wash off the day. When you're done, we'll have dinner and you can tell me what you learned, yeah?"

Leaning into his touch, I relish the tender brush of his thumb along my cheek. Of his scent, something woodsy and fresh with a hint of the sea. I want to ask him to join me. To hold me—naked—and let the hot water wash away everything that could keep us apart. But all I can manage is a whispered, "Okay."

He leaves without a word, and when I'm alone, I turn the water as hot as I think I can stand and shed my bra and panties. The scars across my back stretch tight, and my muscles ache from so long sitting on the frigid ground. The blond wig was unbearably hot, but as soon as I tossed it in a dumpster, my soaking wet hair sapped most of the heat from my limbs.

The hot water starts to cool before I feel clean, and I wrap my body in a thick, forest green towel before opening my backpack and withdrawing a fresh pair of panties and bra. I need to get some new clothes if I'm going to be in Boston for more than a few days. But for tonight, I have one last clean pair of leggings and a flannel shirt.

And socks. Always a fresh pair of socks.

Ronan

Zephyr pads out of the bathroom with a ball of clothing under her arm. "Do you have a washer and dryer?"

In the middle of pouring two pints of Irish Death, I nod toward the closet doors in the hall. "You didn't snoop around last night?"

"No!" Her indignant tone tugs at the corners of my lips. "I took a shower, found your bathrobe, and made myself a cup of tea. I *may* have perused your bookshelf and your fridge. I *definitely* catalogued your entire DVD collection. I've missed a lot of movies the past four years."

"Leave the laundry for later. You found the best pizza place in Boston. It would be a shame to let it get too cold."

After she dumps her clothes into the washer, Zephyr joins me on the couch. "Do you eat all your meals here?" she asks.

"It's only me. Seemed a waste to spend money on a separate table just for eatin'. Half the time, I'm not even home for dinner. You're lucky I have matchin' napkins."

She chuckles, and the way her eyes light up when she laughs? It's mesmerizing. "I don't need matching napkins. Hell, having plates and hot food is a luxury. Don't get me started on the beer."

"Are you sayin' somethin's wrong with my beer?" I ask.

"The opposite." Zephyr lifts the glass to her lips and takes a healthy swig. "Shit. I haven't had a cold pint in forever."

While we eat, I tell her about my conversations with Dax, then Trevor. "This is personal for Dax. He knew Yoden's brother. But he's not an idiot. Trev and Wren are lookin' into the crime scene reports. They'll figure out how the cartel framed you."

"They don't have to," she says softly. "I can tell you everything."

———

THE PIZZA and beer are long gone, the washer provides a calm, reassuring *swish, swish, swish* from the hall, and Zephyr, clad only in one of my t-shirts and panties pats the bed next to her. We turned some sort of corner in the bathroom once I'd seen her scars and practically begged her not to run, and I strip off my Henley and jeans, leaving me in just my boxers before joining her.

"Will you...shit. I'm not good at this." She turns away from me onto her side, but casts a glance over her shoulder. "I've never told anyone what I'm about to tell you. And, I'm scared I won't be able to get through it."

Hold her, you idiot. She's asking you to hold her.

Fitting my body to hers, I let her relax in my arms, trailing my fingers along her hip under the blanket. "I'm here, luv. Why don't you start with why you left the cartel."

Zephyr links her hand with mine. "After François got out of jail, he showed up at Alex's doorstep and the two reconnected. Oliver was still living in the house, but I'd moved out a couple of months earlier. Martín convinced me it was time to get my own place, and I had enough money saved up, I didn't need the family to pay for my everyday expenses."

"How old were you?" Her hair tickles my nose as I press a kiss to the back of her neck.

"Twenty-six. The next couple of jobs...they were normal. We took down an oil magnate who was stealing from his employees' retirement funds. Threatened to send the evidence to the authorities if he didn't pay us ten percent *and* return everything he stole. Alex sent me on a job to recover some art stolen from the Sámi people—I had to break in to the Finnish Museum of Antiquities over a holiday weekend and steal a collection of tools and a couple of pieces of jewelry." She smiles, twisting slightly to meet my gaze. "Hacking into security systems and disabling laser grids? It doesn't get much better than that."

"I think Wren would love you. The two of you together? Unstoppable."

"Is that who you were talking to in Seattle last night?"

Was it only last night? Zephyr's been in my life—in my bed —for less than twenty-four hours, and it doesn't seem real. Like any minute, I'll close my eyes and she'll disappear. "Yes," I say as I tighten my arm around her. "She used to be based here in Boston but moved out to Seattle a couple of years ago. Dax told me she's considered one of the top five hackers in the world."

Zephyr's voice takes on a wistful tone. "I haven't had... friends in four years. The idea that Martín could be in Boston?

That between the two of us, we'd have enough evidence to take down the cartel for good? It seems too good to be true."

"Why isn't your word enough? Because of Yoden?"

She nods. "François and Alex told me Yoden was an arms dealer. The job was to get close enough to clone his mobile, then drug him and leave him in a...compromising position where the press could find him." Her cheeks flush bright red, and she tries to curl away from me, but I won't let her hide. Not anything. Not now.

"Keep goin', luv."

"I begged them to send anyone else but me. Two weeks earlier, I'd told Alex I wanted out. That I needed to make my own way. I'd even found a job. Zenia Vimes had a passport, a lease on a small studio apartment in Vienna, and she was supposed to start work as a technical writer a few days after the Yoden job."

"Zenia?" I try the word out again. "Zenia. It doesn't suit you like Zephyr does, but I like it. Go on, then. You didn't want to do the job."

"I *knew* François was hurting people. The money was rolling in like never before, and there aren't many ways that happens. So I started digging around. The asshole didn't even *try* to hide what he was doing. Drugs, contract killings, guns..." Goosebumps race along Zephyr's arms, and I pull the blankets higher over us. "I copied everything I found to a secure cloud drive and went to Oliver. There was no way I was leaving without my little brother. But..."

She shakes her head, burying her face in the pillow. A single sob shakes her entire body. "Shh, luv. I've got you. Let it out if you need to."

I expect her to break down, to start crying and not stop until there's nothing left in her. But I'm wrong. She takes a few deep breaths, then wriggles around until she's facing me.

"Oliver refused to leave. Said François trusted him with

everything. *Everything.* The look in his eyes, Ronan? He'd already killed. At least three times. The little boy I protected from the streets—the whole reason I joined Alex's family in the first place—I turned him into a killer."

"No!" The word sounds more like a growl, harsher than I intend, but I don't regret it. "You did no such thing. That's on François Strauss. Alex. And Oliver."

She doesn't believe me. Not truly. But a small bit of the guilt in her eyes fades. "I found out later...when they caught me... that Oliver was the one who ratted me out. He told François what I'd done—how I'd made copies of everything—and François sent me on that assignment to kill me."

CHAPTER FOURTEEN

Zephyr

So many memories claw their way to the surface, exploding like a volcano blowing its top until I'm nothing but raw nerves, held together by Ronan's embrace, his warm breath against my neck, his scent surrounding me.

"I only agreed to do the job because Alex promised me it would be the last one. That he needed me. That Yoden was a bad man doing bad things to people, and this was exactly the type of job I excelled at. He practically begged me." My voice threatens to crack, but I clear my throat and clench my hands so hard, my short nails dig into my palms to the point of pain.

"He was like your father," Ronan says, his lips brushing my ear in a gesture so comforting, I want to melt every time he does it. "You couldn't say no."

"I had a sedative prepped, and I stole a housekeeping uniform from the hotel laundry. But he knew I was coming. When he opened the door to his room, he hit me with a tranq dart. I woke up naked and tied to a chair." Stifling my shudder, I shove the overwhelming fear down as far as it will go. So deep when I close my eyes, I'm standing behind Yoden, *watching* him threaten me. "He wasn't an arms dealer at all. He was a professional assassin. And he knew I'd been set up. He actually *warned* me about François."

"Shit. He didn't try to kill you?"

"No." A dry laugh escapes my parched throat, and I wish we were having this discussion over whiskey. But I can't allow myself to get drunk. Impaired judgment could damn us both. "He told me to run. To disappear. That he was giving me this one chance to save myself, but if he ever saw me again, he'd kill me. And then the bastard tranq'd me a second time. I've never had a headache that bad in my entire life. When I came to, he was gone. Took me half an hour to get free."

"So why go to São Paulo?" Ronan plays with a lock of my hair, the teal strands slipping through his fingers over and over again. These little touches mean more than I can possibly explain, and I wish I were brave enough to tell him that.

"Because Oliver begged me to meet him there. They had someone watching me." Shrugging, I continue, "I never found out who. But they knew Yoden hadn't killed me. I thought my brother had come to his senses. That's what he led me to believe. But when I got to the meet, the police were waiting for me. I barely escaped."

My voice is starting to fail. The adrenaline—and tea—that kept me going all day is long gone. Laying my head on Ronan's chest, my arms winding around his waist, I close my eyes. I'll tell him the rest of it. Stay up until dawn if I have to. After a few minutes' rest.

"You're exhausted," he murmurs, pressing a kiss to my temple. His fingers find their way under the t-shirt, skimming my scarred back with the lightest of touches. "Sleep with me, luv. I like having you in my bed."

Forcing my heavy lids open, the truth hits me so fast, it steals the breath from my lungs. I want to *stay* in his bed. Every night. For as long as it's safe. My biggest fear? That 'as long as it's safe' won't last more than another day. Maybe two.

My core clenches at the sight of him. The rough stubble he didn't bother to shave today, the piercing blue eyes, those dark reddish brows and the light dusting of freckles over his nose. He stares at me like I'm this wondrous, precious jewel, and no one has ever made me feel so special. So *wanted*.

He's initiated every kiss. It's my turn now.

Our legs tangle between the sheets, and I wriggle up so we're face to face. "What if I don't want to sleep?"

It doesn't take more than a few seconds for his hard length to press to my hip, and he growls my name. "Zephyr. Fuck. I want you. All of you. But not if I'm to be a balm to soothe yer bad memories."

Framing his cheeks, I lean in and kiss him. At first, it's gentle. Almost hesitant. His words tumble around in my head. Is that what I'm doing? I find my answer when I trace the seam of his lips with a slow sweep of my tongue and he groans.

I pull back just enough for my words to whisper over his skin. "Getting in bed together? Your arms around me? *That* soothed me. Made me feel safe enough to tell you how I ended up here. But this?" Another kiss, bolder this time, and I bite down gently on his bottom lip before I speak again. "This is me doing what *I* want for once. Not what's smart. Not what's going to make it easy for me to run again. This is me showing you I want to stay. With you. That I'll fight for it. For us. For myself."

Ronan rolls me onto my back, pinning me with his leg while he slides his hand into my hair and tightens his grip. "Are you sure, Zephyr? If you're not, we can sleep. Nothin' has to happen."

"I'm sure. For the first time in years, I want something real."

Ronan pulls back the blankets and sits up, his gaze roving from my face all the way to my toes. "You're so damn sexy, I should have you pinch me so I know I'm not dreamin'."

"You're a good liar, mate."

His face hardens, and his voice takes on a rough edge. "I *don't* lie."

The look I shoot him must not land the way I hope, because he rolls out of bed and thrusts his hand toward me. "Come on."

"Where?"

"No questions. You need to trust me."

He has me there. With how many times this subject has come up in the past twenty-four hours, I can't do anything *but* put my hand in his and let him lead me over to the bedroom door.

It shuts with enough force I fight my urge to jump.

A mirror hidden behind it shows me in Ronan's Waterford FC t-shirt with him standing right behind me.

"If you can't see how fuckin' gorgeous you are, I'll show you."

Oh, God. He's not going to...

Grabbing the hem of the t-shirt, he yanks it over my head before I can protest.

Shit.

Two patches of rough, reddish skin mar my stomach on either side of my navel. I try to cover them with my hands, but he captures my wrists and holds on tight.

"Not with me, luv. Your scars don't diminish you one bit. They're evidence you survived. That you're strong. Brave. That you didn't break."

Dropping to one knee, he presses his lips to each of the old burns, then moves to the matching ones on my back.

"I shouldn't be surprised at this," he says after kissing the phoenix inked on my right hip. "It suits you."

My cheeks flame, the color spreading down to my neck and my breasts. Ronan gently turns me partway around and trails kisses up my spine. The position lets me see his face—half of it anyway—and his expression never falters. Nothing but pure admiration and arousal.

Shuddering when his hand cups my breast, I let my eyes flutter closed, enjoying the warmth building in my core until it reaches my heart.

I don't deserve this man, but until he figures that out, I'll memorize the feel of him. Every look. Every touch. Every sensation.

He's on his feet again, tongue and teeth playing along my ear lobe, flicking each of the four hoops as both hands lavish attention on my hard nipples.

"Ronan," I whisper, "please."

"Please? Please what?"

"Bed."

He spins me so I'm facing him and nudges my chin up until I meet his gaze. "Do you believe me now? About how beautiful you are?"

"Yes." I may not understand *why,* but I know he's telling the truth.

Scooping me into his arms with a stifled grunt, he carries me back to the bed. "This isn't goin' to be a quickie, Zephyr. Get comfortable."

I don't try to hide the thrill running through me at his words.

"Back against the headboard," he orders.

"This is suspiciously similar to last night. You're not going to tie me up again, are you?"

His eyes darken. "Not unless you want me to. Bondage isn't my thing. But if it's yours..."

"No." The word flies from my lips, but the moment it does, I wonder. "At least, I don't think so. I've never trusted anyone enough to try."

His palm presses to my cheek, the look in his eyes one I want to see every time he looks at me. "But you trust me?"

"Yes."

With a genuine smile that transforms his ruggedly handsome face into something *more,* he winks at me. "Then maybe one day we try. But not tonight."

Positioning himself between my legs, he hooks his fingers around my panties and tugs them off with a flourish. "You smell like a rain storm, Zephyr. Like I could drown in you and die a happy man."

Before I can respond, he skims his fingers from my knees up my thighs, and I part my legs to afford him better access. The first, quick dart of his tongue over my clit makes me whimper. "Oh, God. Again."

"Liked that, did you?" He laughs, the vibrations ratcheting my arousal another dozen notches. Despite my pleas, he takes his time—alternating bold strokes with light flutters, always stopping to rise up and kiss me moments before I find my release.

Sweat glistens over my entire body, and I ache to have Ronan inside me. "Enough..." I manage. "You...up here...now."

He lifts his head, his lips swollen and glistening with my arousal. "I like you givin' me orders."

Pausing only long enough to snag a condom from his bedside table, he sheds his boxers, and I stare. His body is nothing but wiry muscle, reddish hair, and coiled anticipation.

The foil packet crinkles as he rips it open, and once he's sheathed, he straddles me, grabbing my hips and tugging me down until I'm flat on my back. "Not a disappointment, am I?" he asks, his tip grazing my swollen lower lips.

A hint of fear lends a wobble to his last two words. He's more than average, but from what little experience I've had, there are two types of men in this world. Those who worry they'll somehow disappoint those they care for most and those who think they're the shit. And I'll take the former, no matter what his size, over the latter any day.

"A disappointment? Now who needs to look in the mirror?" I wrap my legs around his hips, and he thrusts deep, filling me in a way no one else ever has. This isn't just "sex." This is more. This is a connection. Two damaged people finding their way home. "Don't be gentle," I say, reaching up and grasping the headboard as he starts to move. "I can take whatever you can give."

His eyes darken at my challenge, and he cants his hips faster. After a moment, I pick up on the rhythm and meet him thrust for thrust, until we're both panting.

"Hold on to me, Zephyr. I want your arms around me... when I come."

He's close, his brow furrowed in concentration, and with every stroke, he gets even harder. I do as he asks, and the position allows enough friction against my clit to send me rushing towards the edge with him.

"Fuck!" he shouts, long and low, and I feel each spasm until my core tightens and I let myself fly.

The world around us softens, muffles, my heartbeat roaring in my ears. I keep my eyes open as long as I can, because what I find in his gaze? It's something I've been searching for my entire life.

Home.

CHAPTER FIFTEEN

Ronan

MY PHONE BUZZES on the nightstand, and I rush to check the screen, hoping Zephyr won't wake up. But she's spent too long on the run. Too long attuned to every sound, and she sits up with the blanket clutched to her chest.

"It's Trevor," I say. "I'll put it on speaker, but you can't make a sound." After she nods, I tap the *Accept* button. "Trev, you're on speaker."

"Clear to talk openly?" he asks.

"Yeah. Just slept in. Ear bud's chargin' in the other room." If we were face to face, Trevor would see through my not-quite-truth easily. But over the phone? I hope he'll trust me.

"Right. I looked into the Yoden murder. Called in a couple of favors. I'm sending some photos to your cloud drive, but the guy in charge of the investigation, Peter Niehaus—"

"Wait, what?" I meet Zephyr's gaze, unsure I heard Trevor correctly. But she's as shocked as I am. "Who's runnin' the investigation?"

"Peter Niehaus. Why?"

"Because the man I've been talkin' to is Dante Lambert. I told him I was headin' to Newbury Street to check out a lead two nights ago, and half an hour later, I get shot?"

"Who the fuck is Dante Lambert?" Trev asks. "None of my contacts mentioned that name."

"I need a minute. Can I put you on hold?" When Trevor agrees, I tap the screen and meet Zephyr's gaze. "If I tell him I'm in contact with you, that Dante Lambert sent you to Boston, we might be able to convince Dax that you're innocent."

"You can't." Zephyr clutches my arm, her eyes wide. "What if they insist you come in? I can't do this without you."

"Trevor will listen. I helped get him out of some trouble last year, and he knows the importance of keepin' secrets." Zephyr trusts *me*, but she doesn't know Trev at all. For her to put her life in *his* hands? That's asking too much, and I know it. But do we have a choice?

"Tell him you found my laptop. It's safer." She scrambles for my Waterford t-shirt and pulls it over her head, then retrieves her panties from the floor.

Fuck. She's getting ready to run. "Zephyr, stay. I can't keep Trevor waitin' much longer, but I won't let him know I can get in touch with you."

The wariness in her eyes hits me hard, but she sits back down next to me, her knees pulled up to her chest.

"I'm back, Trev. Listen, I didn't say anythin' yesterday, but when I found Zephyr's stuff on Newbury Street...that included her laptop."

"Holy fuck. You have to send that to Wren, ASAP." His tone leaves no room for argument, but I have to try.

"Zephyr left it runnin', and I faked her fingerprint to get access. My tech skills are shit, but I didn't need Wren to see her chat history. She's been talkin' to Lambert too. She *trusts* him. He's the one who sent her to Boston. Not to kill, but to track down a former member of the Strauss Cartel who has evidence of their crimes. Lambert's playin' all sides here, Trevor. Sendin' Zephyr into danger, leadin' me to her, and tellin' the cartel where they can find both of us."

Trevor doesn't say anything for several moments, and Zephyr clutches the edge of the blanket so hard, her knuckles turn white. "I'll send out some feelers on Lambert. But call the courier right fucking now and get that laptop to Wren. If you don't, I can't promise anyone will be able to save you from Dax when he finds out you had it for more than a day and didn't say anything."

"Thanks. The rest is in the drop to my cloud drive?" I ask, dancing around the implied order.

"Yes. Take a look, and this afternoon, if you want backup when you talk to Dax, conference me in. Ella's on surveillance for my custody case. Dani sprained her ankle right before she flew back from Mexico last night, so I'm not going in today."

"You need anythin'?" I don't want to leave Zephyr's side for more than five minutes, even though I'll have to when I go to Second Sight. But Trev and Dani are family, and I'd find a way to help. Somehow.

"Nah." Trevor's voice fades, like he's covering the phone speaker with his hand. After a beat, he's back. "She keeps telling me I'm hovering. Doc said she'd be good as new in a few weeks. Until then, she's in a walking boot."

"Tell her that boot's hard enough for her to kick your ass if she has to."

With a laugh, Trevor says goodbye, and I fall back against the pillows.

"This is the proof we needed, luv. Knowin' Dante isn't runnin' the case? Being able to contact the man who is?" I slide my arms around her and pull her on top of me. "We still need to find Martín Levi, but once I bring this all to Dax, we'll have Wren and Ripper's help, and you won't have to hide anymore."

Hope shines in her eyes, but her breath catches in her

throat. "We still have to find Oliver, Theo, and whoever else they have with them. Until then? Every time I step outside—every time *either one of us* steps outside—we're in danger."

She's right, but this is more than I hoped Trevor would find. "Come on. I'll make us tea and we can take a look at the *real* crime scene report."

Zephyr

Our laptops sit side by side on the coffee table, Dante's file on my screen and the *original* report on Ronan's computer.

"Accordin' to Trevor, someone 'altered' the original report two days after the murder and deleted several notes Niehaus added when he toured the scene." He opens a text file with a time stamp less than twenty-four hours after Yoden died and reads the contents out loud.

"The body shows almost no signs of trauma. No offensive or defensive wounds. With the amount of blood in the room, there should be some evidence of a fight."

I snort. "Yoden was a pro. At my best, I might have landed a couple of punches. But he would have taken me down in under a minute. He wasn't vengeful, either. Pull up his kills."

Ronan shoots me a look of utter bafflement.

With a chuckle, I open an encrypted connection to the dark web and start the search. In under five minutes, I have a dozen different photos tiled on screen. "Look at the bodies. Not a single bruise, cut, or scrape other than the killing blows. Ten were shot, two had their throats slit. He was too good. No one could have bested him. And definitely not like...*that.*"

"It's not enough." Ronan finishes his tea and sets the mug down hard. "What about the lab reports? How did they get your DNA and fingerprints? Wren couldn't find anythin' on you besides a handful of passport photos." He scans the case files until he finds the DNA analysis. "Jesus, Mary, and Joseph. There's nothin' there. Just your name, date of birth, and prints."

"That's not my birthday." The words escape before I think them through, and almost immediately, I shake my head. "At least...I don't think it is."

With his brows drawn together, Ronan turns to me. "You don't know your birthday?"

I need more tea. Or some air. Anything to escape this conversation. In the kitchen, I turn on the kettle and brace my hands on the counter. Ronan comes up behind me, winding his arms around my waist. "Talk to me, luv."

"Papa left when I was eleven," I whisper. "I don't know my last name. Or if I have a middle name. He had...problems. I was too young to understand what they were, but I suspect either dementia, early-onset Alzheimer's, or bipolar disorder. Some days he'd be fine. He'd get a part time job and we'd have a picnic at night under the stars. Or he'd come back to the shelter with new clothes for me and Oliver and a big smile on his face."

A tear spills down my cheek, hovers over my jawbone, and then hits the counter with a splash so loud, it's like a waterfall hitting the rocks from a thousand feet.

"We were a family." My voice fades away, and I shatter into pieces so small, the world's best puzzle master couldn't put them back together again. I don't remember sinking down to the floor, or Ronan folding me into his embrace. My eyes burn, but the real pain is in my heart.

Rocking me gently, Ronan makes soft shushing noises in my ear until my sobs turn to quiet sniffles and the occasional hiccup.

"The last birthday I remember," I say, resting my cheek on

his shoulder, "was in the spring. Maybe Papa made it up. He disappeared a month later."

"When this is all over, you can pick a new birthday. Any day you want. And we'll celebrate it every year."

"We?" Another sniffle, and I meet his gaze.

"Yes. We. I'm not goin' anywhere, Zephyr. Last night meant somethin' to me. I care for you. More than I should after knowin' you for less than two days. I'm not walkin' away once we take down the cartel. Not unless you ask me to."

I can't give him the answer he wants. Not even the one *I* want. I can't tell him I care for him too. That he's the kind of man I think I could fall in love with one day. All I can do is nod and let him hold me.

CHAPTER SIXTEEN

Ronan

THE STRONGEST WOMAN I've ever met sobbing in my arms? Nothing in my life has ever made me feel so helpless. Not even getting shot protecting Mikayla.

With an arm around her waist, I guide her into the bathroom and start the shower. Zephyr leans against the counter, her eyes holding none of their usual fire.

"Family isn't just the one you were born with," I say, unsure if I'm helping or hurting as we strip down and step under the spray. "My mum has three kids. But my brother and sister? Their da died three years before I was born. I was...an accident. Mum slept with a man on the third date, and the condom broke. He didn't stick around. Ciara and Cody were a good ten years older than me, and I always felt like the outsider. Mum had to work three jobs to keep us fed, and I grew up...alone, really."

Spilling shampoo into my hands, I start massaging Zephyr's scalp, and the sound she makes? Something between a sigh and a moan? My dick takes notice. But this moment between us is too important, and I can't—I *won't*—let my desire for her come before the connection we're building, so I continue working the suds through her hair.

"After I left the army, I mucked about for a few years, but never found anywhere I thought I fit in. Until I came to Boston."

"A city isn't a family," Zephyr says, her voice so soft, I have to strain to hear her over the water.

"No, but Second Sight is." Angling her so the massaging shower head hits her tense shoulders, I lean in for a long, tender kiss. Zephyr is fast becoming my family too, but she's not ready to hear that yet. "Dax gave me a job with only a single interview. I'd met him when I was deployed, and he said he could tell I had the instincts for the job. I didn't believe him, but what did I have to lose?"

Staring at me like I asked her the daftest question in the world, she arches her brows. "I don't know, mate. What *did* you have to lose?"

Laughing, I switch places with her so I can wash my own hair. "Good point. The answer was nothin'. I didn't want to go back to Ireland, and I needed a job to stay in the U.S. Took a few months, but the men and women I work with started to become a family to me."

"Alex used to say our family was stronger than any blood relations."

Fuck me. A tidal wave of sadness pulls Zephyr under, and she stares at the water swirling down the drain.

"I'm makin' a mess of this," I mutter.

"No. It's not you. It's Alex. François. Oliver. Hell, even *me*. I had two families and lost them both. Maybe I'm meant to be alone."

It's not a question, and my heart aches to comfort her. To

say *anything* that will ease her pain. "Or maybe you needed one more chance." Turning her around, my lips a hair's breath from her ear, I slide my hands around her waist and cross them over her heart. "You can find a family here, luv. With me. With Second Sight." She stiffens, but I don't let her pull away. "There are days I think there's somethin' in the office water. Dax, Ford, Trevor, Wren...hell, Ripper, Graham, West...I could go on. They all found their forevers in the last few years, and no matter how big our family gets, there's always room for one more."

"They'll never accept me," she says, wriggling free. "I'm an assassin, remember? And if that's not enough, the cartel's price on my head will be."

Before I can say another word, she steps out of the shower, wraps herself in a towel, and stalks out of the room.

Damn it. How many more times can I screw up before she walks away for good?

DAX EXPECTS ME AT FOUR, which leaves us six hours to find something more concrete than the altered case files to prove Zephyr's innocence.

"Oliver's on his phone again," she says, and angles her laptop screen toward me.

Oliver: Got a lead on Martín. Forged a warrant and talked to the bank manager. They don't have a physical address for him. Just a PO Box. Going there now to see what I can find.

"Whose number is he texting?" I ask.

"Not positive, but my gut says it's François."

Picking up my tablet, I tap the screen to launch a chat window. "Let me see if Wren can trace either mobile and get us a location."

Zephyr's eyes widen. "No. It's too dangerous. What if she...?"

"Luv, I ask her for traces every case. There's no way she'll know *you* gave me these numbers. Relax. I won't do *anythin'* that would lead Dax or anyone else to you. I'm with you. Til the end."

For several long moments, she stares at me. The doubt in her eyes cuts deep, but then it gives way to another emotion I think might be the early stirrings of love.

"I don't like it, but getting closer to Martín is worth any risk. They'll kill him just as easily and painfully as they'll kill me."

Before I send the message, I let Zephyr read it. Whatever she needs to believe me, to trust that I won't let her down or compromise her safety, she'll have.

Not more than twenty minutes later, Wren responds. *"The first number is pinging off a cell tower between Roxbury and the South End. The second is either off or they're blocking me somehow. Got an ultrasound scheduled for this afternoon, so I'm handing this off to Ripper. If he finds anything more definitive, he'll let you know."*

"She's pregnant?" Zephyr asks.

"Five months. Ryker—that's her husband—is threatenin' to bubble wrap their entire condo. He's former Special Forces and the biggest arse on the planet. But accordin' to Dax, he's scared shitless over the idea of a baby."

Zephyr cracks a weak, sad smile. "Oliver and Jessica wanted kids. I was looking forward to being an aunt."

"You still could be," I say. "In four more months. Though you'll be competin' with at least five other women. That kid is goin' to want for nothin'."

With a shake of her head, she locks her laptop, leaving the facial recognition program running. It's been going for more than twelve hours now, and still no matches to DMV photos from the greater Boston area for the two pictures Zephyr has of Martín. But they're a good seven years old, and the scanner is a dark web unknown.

Zephyr passes me my coat. "We need to go. If Oliver does get Martín's address, we can't be far behind."

Zephyr

The PO Box is in one of the worst neighborhoods in Boston—according to Ronan. The area between Roxbury and the South End is known as Mass and Cass, a haven for drug dealers, addicts, and the homeless.

I bristle at the notion that those without a roof over their heads are somehow...evil...until Ronan reaches over and squeezes my hand. "We've a fair number of people livin' on the streets in the city. The real problem in this neighborhood is roundin' up the dealers and gettin' help to those who need it. Second Sight hired a whole mess of Rent-a-Cops to accompany social workers down there this past September. We got a couple hundred people into shelters, treatment centers, or at least to better, safer encampments. It's not enough, but we'll do it again in the spring."

"Some of the places we lived—before Papa disappeared—were horrible," I admit. "But most were filled with good people in a bad way." The prospect of running into Oliver has my nerves on overdrive, and I twist the tiger's eye ring around and around on my thumb until Ronan notices.

"You've not worn that before."

"It was Papa's. All I have left of him. The day he disappeared, I found it on my pillow. It's how I knew he wasn't coming back." The golden brown stone shimmers in the harsh, winter's light, but it's warm to the touch. "I haven't felt...safe enough to wear it since I left the cartel. Until now." His smile sends goosebumps racing down my arms. "Ronan? I trust *you*. I know you need me to trust your boss. Your coworkers. And I'm not there yet. But I'm trying."

He steals glances at me as we reach the border between the South End and Roxbury, the silence in the car almost too much for me to bear. Until he finds a parking spot three blocks from Boston Mail Center and shuts off the engine. "You're doin' just fine, luv. It's me who's bein' an arse. Never met anyone like you. I'm gone for you, and that makes me a bit…overprotective."

"A bit?" Laughing, I tug the wool cap down over my hair. We stopped at a drug store on the way, and I touch up the purple lipstick that matches the polarized sunglasses hiding my eyes. With Ronan's leather jacket covering a Boston Red Sox t-shirt, I hope I look different enough Oliver won't immediately recognize me.

"Stay close," Ronan says. We're both armed. A belt holster holds his Glock 19, and he has a backup piece at his ankle. He had to cinch all the straps, but managed to get his shoulder harness to fit me so I can carry his Sig Sauer P238.

If I didn't need my hands free, I'd tuck my arm in his. I want to stay *more* than close. Locked in Ronan's apartment for a solid week sounds perfect right now. Aruba would be nice too. A beach, a bungalow, some silly drinks with umbrellas in them. All things I've never allowed myself to want, because what good are they when you have no one to share them with?

Now, this handsome, gruff man at my side is talking about family and forevers, and everything I've ever dreamed of.

Suddenly, Ronan spins me around and presses me up against the wall of a used bookstore. Before I can protest, he angles his head to plant a kiss to the side of my neck. "The shithead who shot me is at my five o'clock. Don't see your brother yet."

Hooking my leg around his, I grab his ass and dig my fingers into the firm muscles under his black pants. "The mailbox place is on the next corner. Can you reach my phone?

See if he's texted Theo?" His hand slides into my back pocket for the device while I keep one eye on Theo until the man turns and starts walking the other way. "He's heading south. You can stop with the groping."

"You mean to tell me you didn't enjoy that?" He cracks a brief smile and passes me the phone.

"Oh, I did. Very much. Except the part where I can't tear your clothes off because we're outside, in winter, with two people who want me dead a block away." Despite my words, I grin up at him. "Tonight, I want you at least twice."

"Your wish is my command, luv."

"Shit. According to Oliver, they didn't get an address from the PO Box, but they did manage to grab a pile of mail. They're heading back to the car now. If we can get their license number..."

"Wren can track it," Ronan finishes. "Come on, then. Feel like runnin'?"

Before he finishes asking the question, I'm already hoofing it to the corner. Oliver's nowhere to be seen, but Theo ducks into an alley mid-block. "Check the store. Oliver hasn't seen your face yet—not well enough anyway. I'm going after Theo."

"No. We stay together," he growls.

"I won't get too close. But if we lose both of them...we won't have any hope of getting a license number. Go!" I shove at him, angling my hands at the last minute to avoid his injured shoulder. He's pissed, but nods and crosses the street, while I rush toward the alley.

Stopping two steps from the alley against an old, half-abandoned building, I take a quick peek around the corner. Hands grab my jacket, spinning me and throwing me against the opposite building's wall. Rough concrete scrapes my cheek and the sunglasses shatter.

Fuck.

I can't get to the gun before Theo's on me again. The idiot's huge—easily three-hundred pounds of solid muscle. Unable to fight momentum, I crash into the other wall. Sparks zing where my elbow catches a pipe protruding from the concrete, but this time when he comes for me, I'm ready.

Kicking my leg out behind me, I catch him in the balls, and he squeals like a little kid. "Didn't know you had anything left down there, asshole," I taunt, grabbing his shoulders and driving my knee into his nose. The crunch shouldn't be so satisfying, but after all the pain he caused me, I need a little payback. "Steroids really do a number on those little raspberries, I hear."

Shoving him as hard as I can, I expect him to go down, but he staggers back until he hits the wall, then uses it as leverage, tackling me and driving the breath from my lungs.

His massive fingers wrap around my throat, but before he cuts off my air, I grab his wrist with both hands and wrench it downward, breaking his hold. I use my whole body to knock him onto his side.

The wail of a police siren approaches. Shit, shit, shit. A quick glance onto the street and I know why. A man holds his cell phone at eye level, recording our entire fight.

He's too far away to get a clear shot of my face, but that won't matter if the police catch me. Theo takes off at a dead run, and before I can decide whether to follow him or go back the way I came, footsteps pound closer.

"Zephyr!" Ronan's rough whisper sends relief flooding through me, but it's short lived. He tosses me the car keys as he rounds the corner. "The cops are half a block away. Start runnin'. I'll meet you back at the car as soon as I can, but don't expect it to be for at least half an hour." He's blocking me from view of the camera man and holds his hands up. "Don't shoot!" he shouts. "I'm no threat to you!"

Spinning on my heel, I take off in the same direction as Theo, and pray he's so worried about the cops, he won't even *think* about trying for round two.

Ronan

After the police run my PI license and call Second Sight to verify I'm still employed—a question that made me hold my breath until Marjorie relayed Dax's answer—I give a quick statement.

"I heard shoutin' and sounds of a fight, so I came to see if anyone needed help. Saw a big bloke runnin' down the alley. He turned left. The woman pulled a gun. I put my hands up, told her I wasn't after her, and she backed away a dozen steps or so, then bolted."

"Can you describe her, Mr. Murphy?" the officer asks.

"Caucasian. Five-five, maybe a hundred and thirty pounds. She had on a black cap and a black leather jacket. Didn't see much else but the gun. Nice arse as she was runnin' away."

Officer Verti chuckles. "And the man?"

"Only saw him from the back at a distance. Big guy. Taller than me. If he's not a fighter somewhere, he should be. Jeans, dark brown shirt. Black hair. Pretty sure he was Caucasian too, but I only caught a glimpse of his hands so I can't be sure."

If the guy across the street hadn't been filming the whole damn fight, I could have given the police a full description of Theo. But as soon as they see the video, they'll know there's no way I could have seen his face. Every minute I spend away from Zephyr it's harder to concentrate, but if I lose the narrative, we could both be in a world of hurt.

"If we need to contact you again?" the officer asks.

I rattle off my office direct line, and Verti scribbles it in his notebook. "Call anytime. I hope you find both the man and the woman."

The trip back to the car takes me a full fifteen minutes. I stop at a little convenience store a block away, perusing the aisles and checking for tails before I buy a couple of candy bars and make a beeline for Zephyr.

I don't see anyone in the car as I approach, and my heart shoots into my throat until I reach the door. The cuff of one of my jacket sleeves pokes out from between the rear seats.

"It's me," I say when I open the door. The left rear seat folds down, and Zephyr wriggles out from the trunk.

"Thank God. I *hate* small, dark spaces. And your jack was digging into my side. I feared if I shifted my weight, the whole car would move." Her cheek bears a fresh scrape, and fingertip bruises are starting to swell around her throat.

"Dammit, Zephyr. He could have taken you. Or killed you right in that alley!" The second she's sitting across from me, I pull her into my arms and hold on tight. "I knew splittin' up was a bad idea. Oliver wasn't at the PO Box anymore, and I didn't get a chance to check out the area because of the sirens."

"I'm sorry," she says, her breath warm on my neck. "I was careful. Stopped a couple of steps away from the corner, but as soon as I tried to get a look down the alley, Theo grabbed me. I don't know when he saw me or how, but he knew I was there."

My phone rings before I can say anything else, and I groan. "It's Dax. He's...goin' to be pissed. Stay quiet."

"Dax, this wasn't like—"

"Get your ass in here right fuckin' now. A fight in one of the worst neighborhoods in Boston, and from the video posted online, the woman was Zephyr. You better have a damn good explanation for why she's not sitting in my office in cuffs or you'll be back to stakeouts starting tomorrow morning."

The call ends before I can reply, and I meet Zephyr's gaze. "This is goin' to be bad. I'll drop you at home on the way, and you need to promise me you won't step foot outside the apartment."

"I promise." She pulls her knees up to her chest and hugs herself tightly. Adrenaline crash, if I had to guess, and I wish I could stay with her. Hold her. Take care of her. But if I don't report in, Dax will come looking for me, and that wouldn't end well for anyone.

CHAPTER SEVENTEEN

Ronan

"You *had her*. Staring right at her and you couldn't get the gun away from her? You expect me to believe that?" Dax braces his hands on his desk, and I wonder—briefly—if he's doing that so he doesn't leap over the damn thing and strangle me.

"No."

It's not the answer he expects, and he straightens with a frown. "Then what happened?"

"Before I say anythin', I'll ask for your word that you'll let me finish before you murder me."

His entire demeanor switches, the anger turning to something closer to betrayal. "You're a member of this team, Ronan. This *family*. No one's murdering anyone on my watch."

The words sting, as does his tone, and I sink down into the guest chair and wait for Dax to take a seat behind the desk. "I let her go. She's innocent. The Strauss Cartel set her up for Yoden's murder because she has dirt on them. A lot of it. The contact you gave me from the General Intelligence and Security Service? He doesn't exist. Or at least, he's not attached to the case in any way. Dante Lambert is playin' both sides. He's the one who convinced Zephyr to come to Boston in the first place, and he's hedgin' his bets by gettin' us to go after her too. If I bring her in, the cartel will get to her within hours, and they'll torture her until she gives them what they want."

Dax waits several seconds before he asks, "Are you finished?"

"Yeah. I'm done."

"Did you *ever* get close enough to take her into custody?"

If I lie, he'll know. I told Zephyr this might happen when I dropped her at my apartment, and she knows to run if I don't call or text her in the next hour with the code word "angel."

"Yes. But she told me she didn't land in São Paulo until three days after Yoden was killed, and Wren verified customs records. She wasn't there. Trevor made some calls to his CIA contacts and that's when I found out Lambert wasn't who he claimed to be. I've been workin' *with* Zephyr for two days, tryin' to track down another former cartel member she believes can corroborate her testimony about a legion of crimes perpetrated by François Strauss and half a dozen others over the past nine years."

A vein in Dax's neck throbs, and I'm no longer convinced my brilliant idea is anything but pure, unadulterated shit.

"I'm tempted to revoke your promotion right fucking now for disobeying a direct order, but if I gave you bad intel, then this is partly on me. I stand by my earlier statement about murder being against office policy, but I need to know one thing." He takes off his glasses, and though it's obvious his eyes can't focus, they're trained on whatever vague shape of me he *can* see.

"What?"

"Would you bet your life on her innocence?"

I don't hesitate. "Yes. Zephyr has never killed anyone. She was set up, and she's in mortal danger if we don't help her."

Dax pinches the bridge of his nose, his eyes closed, and heaves out a breath. "All right. You have twenty-four hours to bring her into this office."

"Dax—"

"I said 'bring her into this office.' Not arrest her, not turn her over to the authorities. Not cuff her and drag her kicking and screaming. Convince her to come in and tell her story. Pull in Wren and Ripper. Verify as much as you can. We don't turn away the innocent here, but there's a fuckton of evidence pointing to her guilt. If she needs our help, she'll have it. But if she's somehow conned you into believing a lie...you're on desk duty for the next century."

Do I thank him? Tell him I'll do my best? I can't give him my word. Not without talking to Zephyr first.

"Well? What are you waiting for? Get out of here," Dax says. "You have work to do."

Zephyr

Every instinct tells me to run, but my heart won't let me. Ronan called and gave me the code word half an hour ago, then said he'd be back with takeout soon. Most importantly, he assured me Dax believed him enough we'll be safe here tonight.

I wish I knew what that meant. Will the police storm the apartment first thing in the morning? I'm starting to get comfortable here. *Too* comfortable.

My toothbrush sits in a cup with Ronan's on the bathroom counter. I bought my own deodorant, shampoo, and conditioner today when we stopped at the mini-mart for my now-destroyed sunglasses.

This morning, I handed Ronan two hundred dollars, and he let me use his credit card to order a ten-pack of panties, two pairs of jeans, three bras, and a pair of shoes whose primary function *isn't* traction or stealth.

I'm turning into someone who wants...*more*. And that's a dangerous thing.

My laptop beeps from the coffee table. Perfect. I start the screen capture software and bring up the chat window.

Dante: You have been offline for twenty-four hours. I was starting to worry.

Zephyr: The bank was a dead end. But that's not the worst thing to happen in the past day. Some asshole private investigator is after me. He's the one who has my laptop, and he managed to get my fingerprint somehow to unlock it.

Dante: What does he have access to? Can he see this chatroom?

Zephyr: When have you ever known me to be that stupid? He knows I was trying to hack into the DMV and he probably found Martín's alias, Michael Lawrence. But unless he can guess a sixteen-word passphrase in three tries or less, he'll never see Martín's photos on my encrypted cloud drive.

Dante: Who is he?

Zephyr: His name is Ronan Murphy. I lifted his wallet this morning. Can you use your General Intelligence and Security Service databases to get me his phone number? If I can run a trace on his mobile, I'll be able to track his location. At least from cell tower to cell tower.

Dante: I will see what I can do. Give me a few hours. Keep your head down and do not get careless. You do not know how many people may be after you.

The connection drops, and I sink back against the cushions and blow out a long, slow breath. "You're right about that one, asshole. For all I know, François brought the whole family to hunt me down."

Turning the screen capture off, I wander to the living room

window and stare out at the city through the privacy glass. It's almost dusk, the trees casting long, leafless shadows across the sidewalks. A few snowflakes drift to the ground on a gentle breeze.

Will I see Christmas in Boston? Or...at all? Does Ronan celebrate? He's Irish. He's probably Catholic. Will he buy a tree? Fresh cut or fake? Egg nog? Candy canes?

"Stop it," I mutter to my reflection in the glass. "None of this matters if you can't find Martín and clear your name. Stop dreaming and get back to work."

THE DOOR LOCKS DISENGAGE, and I'm on my feet before Ronan takes two steps into the apartment. "Did you buy out an entire restaurant?"

His laugh doesn't hold its usual mirth, and tiny lines tighten around his eyes. "Not the whole place, no."

I try to ease two of the four large bags from his hands, but he shakes his head. "Go relax. This meal came with strict platin' instructions. Do you like wine?"

"We have work to do." In truth, I'd kill for a drink, but losing my edge isn't an option.

"One glass. If you don't like Chardonnay, I'll make you tea." For reasons I don't understand, this meal is important to him. If I hadn't been daydreaming about spending Christmas with Ronan less than an hour ago, I'd ask him to explain, but instead, I smile.

"I like Chardonnay. But no getting drunk for either of us." Leaning in for a quick kiss, I get a whiff of something rich and creamy, and my stomach growls. "Oh, God. I don't care what's in those bags, I want it."

Some of the tension drains from his face, and his eyes soften. "We'll need a bit of room."

"Okay, Mr. Mysterious. But if you wait too long to tell me everything that happened with your boss, I might implode."

"Wouldn't want that," he says, a hint of a smile tugging at his lips. "Can you wait until after the first course?"

"The *first* course? Damn, Ronan." Backing away, I wait until the last moment to turn around, but he doesn't make a move until I'm seated on the couch with the kitchen wall between us.

The smells wafting toward me keep getting better and better, and I lean forward, hoping to catch a glimpse of whatever it is, to no avail.

After what feels like forever, Ronan sets a chilled bottle of Chardonnay on a placemat in front of me, followed by two glasses. "I trust you to pour, luv." With a wink, he retreats to the kitchen again.

I haven't had wine in almost a year. Assuming I'm somewhere safe, I treat myself to a glass on the anniversary of my "freedom date" from the cartel, but that's the only indulgence I've risked in ages.

When the steaming bowl of clam chowder appears in front of me, I glance up at Ronan, unable to stop the tears from pricking my eyes.

"I saw the way you looked at the Chowder Shack this afternoon. You might have drooled a little."

Sitting close enough our thighs touch, he picks up his glass. "We're goin' to get through this, Zephyr. I know it like I know my own name. But in case things get rough before the end, I wanted to take you on a proper date. We can't go out, so I brought the date here."

I don't cry. Before this week, I haven't shed a tear in…as long as I can remember. But this man—this amazing, romantic, handsome man—is turning me into someone I don't recognize. Someone with wants. Needs. *Desires.* All of which could get me killed. And yet…a tear spills over. "Two days ago, you were ready to shoot me."

He leans in, dashing the tear away with his thumb. "No one's perfect, luv. I don't know why you trusted me or why you stayed. But I'll do everythin' I can to keep you safe, and here. With me."

I want to believe him. Sink into everything he has to offer like I'm a normal woman—one not wanted for murder—and there's a future for us beyond these walls. But I'm not, and we both know it.

Still, I can pretend. For an hour. Or a day. So I melt into his touch and smile.

"I believe you. Now, let's eat."

CHAPTER EIGHTEEN

Ronan

WATCHING Zephyr during the meal is like seeing a kid on Christmas morning. She savors every bite of Boston's best clam chowder, of the perfectly medium-rare filet mignon, the steamed vegetables, and moans when she samples the cheese-cake for dessert.

By the time I clear the last of the plates and load the dish-washer, she's reclining on the couch, eyes closed.

"I was wrong. The wine wasn't the dangerous part of the meal. I think this is what's called a 'food coma'?"

Laughing hurts. I'm stuffed full, and she's right. "We could go to bed right now and I'd be a happy man." With two cups of tea in my hands, I join her on the couch. "Though I seem to remember you sayin' somethin' about wantin' me naked."

She chuckles but forces her eyes open and grins. "I do. But not until later. Vomiting isn't sexy."

Snuggling against me, her head on my shoulder, Zephyr sighs. "You never told me about the meeting with your boss."

Over dinner, we stuck to lighter subjects. Favorite books,

the movies she missed, all those "normal" first date conversations—through the lens of a fugitive from, well…everyone.

I fill her in, sharing every detail. She deserves my complete honesty, even if she's angry with me in the end. But she's *not* angry. She's scared, and that makes me feel even worse.

"So what happens tomorrow?" she asks, a hint of a wobble to her voice.

"We bring everythin' we have to Second Sight." Taking her hands in mine, I wait for her to meet my gaze. "I swear, Zephyr, if you feel uncomfortable at any time, I'll get you out of there."

"How? Aren't all the people you work with badasses?"

Even though she has a point, I'm not worried. Much. "They are. But I have somethin' they don't." She arches her brows, waiting for my answer. "You mean everythin' to me. There is no possible way Dax, Ford, or Trevor could stop me if I had to protect you."

"Determination only gets you so far," she says. "Physical prowess still counts for something."

"That it does." I wish I had the words to tell her the depth of my feelings for her. But even if I did, it's too soon. I'd spook her, and I won't take that risk.

Zephyr sits up, a quiet "oof" accompanying the movement. "Theo landed a couple of good blows." She rubs her shoulder gently. "Thank God men have a built-in weak spot."

"You got him in the mickey?"

"Mickey? Sometimes you are *so* Irish." With a gentle nudge of her thigh against mine, she smiles.

"Would you want me any other way?"

"Never." Reaching for her laptop, she shows me the conversation she had with Dante this afternoon. "If he comes back without your number, we've caught him in one lie. But it's not enough. We need more."

The info Trevor sent over cycles through my head on a loop. "Wren is searchin' for his name in all the known dark web intelligence databases, and Peter Niehaus is going to find out if he's *ever* worked for the General Intelligence and Security Service."

"Still not enough to prove he's in with the cartel." Her eyes unfocused, she stares out the window. Snowflakes sparkle in the glow of the street lights, and if it keeps up at this rate, the city will be blanketed in white by morning. "Call him," she says. No longer mired in her food coma, she sits up straight and meets my gaze. "Ask him for more information on me. My age. Height. Eye color. Weaknesses."

"I hardly think you have any of those, luv. You're the strongest woman I've ever known."

She laughs, a sound I've come to crave. "To my own credit, I *am* a badass bitch. But this is a test. If Dante is in contact with the cartel, he'll be able to tell you that I'm thirty-four. Five-foot-five. Green eyes. I wear contacts for every passport photo. Never green. Gray, blue, brown, hazel. Even went heterochromic once. But never straight green."

"And your weaknesses?" I'm baffled. In all the tense situations we've been in these past few days, she's been nothing but a rock.

Her shoulders curl inward, and she wraps her arms around herself. "François and Alex would know of two." Blowing out a slow breath, she swallows hard. "I'm terrified of small, dark places."

"You're claustrophobic?"

"Not...exactly." As if she's desperate to prove she's not currently trapped somewhere small and dark right now, she pushes to her feet and starts to pace my living room. "Between Theo's *interrogation* sessions, they'd lock me in this old shipping trunk." Her voice cracks, and she clears her throat, never looking directly at me. "I couldn't sit up or straighten my legs. It smelled...old. Like dust and mold and decay. Even though it wasn't air tight, it felt like it was. Every time they dumped me in there, I had a panic attack so extreme, I'd pass out. Then wake up still locked inside, and panic all over again. It was exhausting, and a hundred times worse than what happened when they pulled me out."

Shit. I'm going to tear Theo apart, piece by piece. Or make him suffer the same horrors he inflicted on Zephyr for much, much longer. She's shaking, her chest stuttering with each breath, and though I'm not sure she wants to be touched, I can't sit here and watch her fall apart in front of me.

Approaching slowly, my hands at my sides, I keep my voice soft. "Can I hold you, luv?"

A single jerk of her head is all she can manage before she launches herself at me. She doesn't cry. Doesn't break down. Doesn't say a word. But she clings to me like I'm her only tether to sanity.

"I've got you. I'll *always* have you."

IT TAKES her half an hour to stop shaking, and when we return to the couch, she's subdued, her cheeks so pale, I wish I could wrap her in a blanket and fall asleep in front of the fire. "What do you need right now?" I ask.

"To work." Zephyr pulls her computer into her lap. "I'm hacking my way through Boston National's firewalls to see if I can find any information on Martín. Oliver said he couldn't get his address or phone number, but who knows what the bank has that they wouldn't turn over, even in the face of a warrant."

She's so focused, I grab my phone and move to the window. Dante picks up on the second ring. "Ronan. Any news on the assassin?"

"She's squirrelly. Been close to her multiple times in the past few days, but she keeps slippin' away. Need to ask you a couple of questions if you have a moment?"

"Of course." He's so smug, I want to punch him through the phone. Or tell him I know he's dirty as fuck.

"There's precious little we know about her. Do you have any hard details? Age? Height? Eye color? And any weaknesses. I need an edge. Anythin' you can give me."

"I am getting another call that I must take right now. May I send you an email message with this information?"

"That would be brilliant. Thank you." He hangs up mid-sentence, and I snort. "He's either spooked and knows we're on to him or he's about to contact someone in the cartel."

Zephyr looks up briefly. "What happened?"

"He said he'd email me. Claimed he had another call he had to take." Heading for the kitchen to make a fresh pot of tea, I call over my shoulder, "If he'd truly been the case officer in charge, he'd have ready answers to all my questions. He's stallin' so he can get them."

"I'm in!" Zephyr announces, pumping her fist and grinning at me when I peer around the kitchen wall. "At the bank. Get over here. Let's see what we can find on Martín—aka Michael Lawrence."

The fire is back in her eyes, thank God, and as soon as the tea's ready, I join her. "I can't wait for you to meet Wren. She's goin' to love you."

Her shoulders stiffen for a brief moment before she forces out a breath. "I hope that happens," she says softly. "That I'm still *here* after tomorrow. Or...anywhere."

"You will be." The urge to give her my promise clogs my throat, but before I can clear it, Zephyr clicks on a file with Michael Lawrence's name on it.

"Yes!" she hisses, almost to herself. "Got a phone number."

Holy shit. It's right there in black and white. The PO Box number and address the bank manager gave to Oliver are at the top of the file, but in a notes field at the bottom, a Boston-based phone number.

"Call him. Right now, luv. You have to warn him the cartel's comin' for him. I can get a team to any address in the city in a little over an hour. If he wants to come in, he'll be protected."

The look she shoots me? It might just be love.

Zephyr

With my phone on the table in front of us, I dial what I hope is Martín's number. Since Dante was the one who told me his alias, I can't be positive, but why else would Oliver and Theo want to find him?

"Who is this?"

I'd know the raspy male voice with a hint of a French accent anywhere. Martín taught me so much over the years. Knots—and how to escape them—how to fool facial recognition algorithms, hotwire a car, pick locks...

Every bit of practical, hands-on knowledge I have? He influenced all of it.

"It's Zephyr."

The call disconnects immediately, and the overwhelming frustration and disappointment threaten to pull me under.

"That was him, yeah?" Ronan asks. Strong fingers stroke up and down my thigh, and I grab his hand, needing an anchor in all this chaos.

"Yes. I lived in the same house with him for more than ten years. I'd know his voice anywhere."

"Maybe he doesn't know you left?"

I don't want to dash his hope. Probably because I don't have any left of my own. But I have no choice. "He knows. He's the one who told me about all the bad shit François was into. He made me promise to leave, and when I did...he sent me a message. One sentence. 'I'm proud of you.'"

"Try again. Maybe you surprised him. Maybe he didn't know what to say."

There's that hope again. The man has it in spades, and I can't muster enough to pick up the phone. Ronan has to dial for me, but the call goes straight to voicemail.

"Would he trust you more if he saw your face?" Ronan asks. "Trevor's an expert at readin' micro expressions. He can tell when someone's lyin' to him by how fast they blink, their speech patterns, where they're lookin'."

"You expect him to pick up a video call?" I huff out a laugh. "He's definitely *not* going to do that."

His hands cup my shoulders gently, and the contact settles me. "Then text him a recordin'. Zephyr, what do you have to lose?"

Nothing. If Martín can't help me, my life is probably over.

I don't say the words aloud. Ronan would freak out. Or he'd spend the rest of the night trying to convince me I'm wrong.

"What the hell. Worst case, he deletes it immediately. But I need a blank wall. Somewhere he can't tell where I am."

None of Ronan's walls are decorated. It's a damn good thing he only moved in a month ago. In the entry hall, he holds the phone up and nods when he taps the record button.

"I know it's you," I begin. "I'll never forget your voice. Or everything you taught me. Like the code word. Violets. You're the reason I'm still alive. But I've been running for years, and I'm tired. I'm in Boston. Someone betrayed me, and the cartel's here too. You know what will happen if they find us. Help me. Between the two of us, we have enough evidence to take them down for good. I can get that intel to people who know what to do with it. *Good* people. People I trust. People who'll protect both of us. You have my number. Please...call me."

Ronan ends the recording, and I text it to Martín. Now, all we can do is wait.

CHAPTER NINETEEN

Ronan

A LITTLE AFTER 10:00 p.m., Wren calls. I angle my tablet so she won't be able to see Zephyr and tap the screen. "Did you find anythin'?"

"Hello to you too, Ronan," Wren says with a frown.

Running a hand through my hair, I want to kick myself. Wren works whenever we need her—even now with constant morning sickness. "Sorry. It's been a long day. Are you feelin' all right?"

Her voice softens, and she scoots back from the screen and cradles her baby bump. "I felt her kick at the doctor's this morning. She was super active during the ultrasound, and I finally figured out I wasn't...err...gassy. She's been kicking for at least a week now."

"That's amazin', Wren. Has Ry felt her move yet?"

Ryker McCabe passes through the video frame, pausing to give me a hard stare. "No, dammit," he growls. "Our kid is going to hate me."

"She will not!" Wren leans back and snags Ryker's wrist,

tugging him closer and placing his palm on her belly. "Just wait while I give Ronan an update on the assassin case."

"It's *not* the assassin case. Zephyr's never killed anyone," I snap. "She's innocent, and the Strauss Cartel is going to kill her if we can't—"

"Watch your tone, asshole." Ryker rounds the leather couch and takes a seat, his hand never moving from Wren's bump. "It was the assassin case when Dax asked Wren to put the first dossier together. She's been working for six hours straight, trying to untangle all the new shit you threw at her—"

"Ry? I can fight my own battles, remember?" Wren pats his hand. "And this is *my* case. Not yours. Sit still and look pretty."

Across the couch, Zephyr claps her hand over her mouth, and I laugh so hard I have to prop the tablet on the coffee table so I don't drop the damn thing.

"Do you have a death wish, Ronan?" Ry asks. "If so, by all means, keep laughing."

That cuts the laughter to an occasional snicker. Wren rolls her eyes, then taps her keyboard a few times. The screen splits in two, a man's photo on the left and Wren on the right. "Meet Dante Lambert. He's a junior data analyst at the General Investigation and Security Service in Antwerp."

Zephyr sits up straight, her eyes wide. God, I wish I could tell Wren about her. The two speak the same language, and together...they'd untangle this mess in no time.

"Uh, Ronan?" Wren asks, killing the split screen and leaning closer to the camera. "For fudgsicles' sake. Move the tablet so Zephyr can see what we're talking about."

In under two seconds, Zephyr's on her feet. Fear steals all the color from her cheeks. She's ready to bolt, and I don't blame her.

"How...?" I ask.

Now it's Wren's turn to laugh. "Seriously? You're sitting *sideways* on your couch. That can't be comfortable."

"A piece of advice," Ry says. "Don't *ever* play poker unless you're prepared to lose *a lot* of money."

"Come on, luv," I say, then cringe. Wren and Ry don't need to know how I feel about Zephyr. It's bad enough they know she's here. "You...uh...didn't hear that."

"Hear what?" Wren grins, then elbows Ry in the arm. "I told you."

Zephyr sits back down, and I scoot closer to her and turn the tablet so we're both on screen. She reaches for my hand, just out of the frame, and holds on tight. "Um, hi?"

"You can't tell anyone she's here. Dax gave me until tomorrow afternoon..."

"We know." Wren splits the screen again. "Dante Lambert joined the security service a year before Yoden's assassination, but he's never been attached to the investigation. His personnel records indicate he's been reprimanded a dozen times for general..."

"Fuckery," Ryker supplies.

"Hush." A new photo appears on screen, this one grainy, but very obviously Zephyr. "Stockholm, the day of Yoden's murder. Pretty safe to say Zephyr wasn't anywhere near São Paulo. Unless she figured out how to teleport, in which case, Ry and Dax are going to hire her on the spot."

"Will that stand up in court?" I ask. "Is it enough?"

"I can send this to Peter Niehaus right now." Wren angles her gaze at Zephyr. "If you're okay with that. If not, I'll keep it between us."

"You're asking *me*?" Zephyr shakes her head. "I don't understand."

Wren smiles. "Second Sight and Hidden Agenda—that's the K&R firm Ry started out here in Seattle—we don't keep secrets. And we don't go behind each other's backs. I realize you don't have any reason to trust me, but it's the truth."

"Ronan's the first person I've trusted in...years. It's not...easy for me." Squeezing my fingers to the point of pain, she sucks in a long, slow breath. "If Niehaus gets that photo, how do we know Dante won't see it too? If he finds out I have help..."

"Leave that to me," Ryker says. "I'll call Pritchard. Have him make contact with Niehaus. Wren can send him the photo on a backchannel."

"Pritchard?" Zephyr shoots me a fearful look. "Who's...Pritchard?"

"Stars and Bars was the head of the Joint Special Operations Command. He's got clout. Even now." Ryker's about to get up, but Wren stops him.

"Hand on the bump, tough guy. You can wait five minutes to call Austin," Wren says. "This baby is going to kick soon and you're *going* to feel it. End of discussion."

Ry grumbles something unintelligible and with his free hand, pulls out his phone and starts texting.

Wren moves his fingers slightly lower before returning her focus to us. "Zephyr? Ronan said you had information that could take the cartel down. I don't need to know what it is or where it is, but is it safe?"

"Yes. I have an encrypted cloud storage account with a sixteen-word passphrase. One fully mirrored backup storage account, same level of security, but different passcode."

Wren's jaw drops for a split second. "Spitsnacks. Ry? You, Dax, or Austin need to hire her right flipping now."

"Spitsnacks?" Zephyr asks. "What the hell?"

"Wren doesn't swear. Much. You get used to it. And I told you she'd love you." Bringing our joined hands to my lips, I brush a kiss to her knuckles. Fuck hiding. Wren and Ryker guessed my feelings for her in under a minute, and I'm not wasting any more time.

"You're hired," Ryker says. "You can decide who you work for when this is all over. Or tell us all to fuck off. After the cartel's *taken care of*, your life is your own."

Zephyr swallows hard, and her eyes crinkle with pain. Shit. I didn't even think her neck might be sore after Theo tried to strangle her earlier today. Her voice isn't steady, but she meets Wren's gaze through the screen. "I don't know what to say."

"Right now, all you have to do is come up with a contingency plan for that data." Wren fiddles with her keyboard and initiates a file transfer to my tablet. "I'm sending Ronan a temporary passkey to a file share only I have access to. Full disclosure, Cam, who's married to West, who works for Ry, is *my* contingency should anything happen to me."

"Contingency?" Zephyr asks.

"If I die. Or for when I have the baby and have to be out of commission for a few hours." She's so matter-of-fact, but Ryker's eyes harden.

"Sweetheart—"

"Ry, I'm *fine*. The baby's *fine*. But you know it's stupid not to plan for this stuff. Calm down. Now, Zephyr, if you decide to upload a copy there, be aware it'll log your IP address and location unless you mask them, but I'm guessing you know how to do that."

"I do. You'll make sure it gets to the right people? If..."

"Shh, luv. Nothin' is goin' to happen to you. We'll go to Dax with all of this tomorrow. Wren? Can you check traffic cams in a three block radius around Harold and Monroe? We're lookin' for Zephyr's brother, Oliver, and a piece of shit named Theo. Theo and Zephyr had a dust up in an alley at 2:45 p.m., and Theo ran off, presumably toward their car. We need to know where they're hidin' out so we can put an end to them."

"On it," she says, scribbling on a piece of paper. "It'll take a bit. Doctor doesn't want me working more than eight hours a day, but I'll do what I can tonight and then pass it off to Ripper or Cam. I won't tell them what it's for, Zephyr. I promise."

The woman I'm falling for looks to me, and it's so easy to read the question in her eyes. *"Can I trust her?"*

"Wren has very strong opinions on the words 'I promise'. She doesn't use them unless she means them. None of us do." Giving her hand another quick squeeze, I wait for her to decide if she's willing to trust one more person.

It only takes another beat for her to nod. "Okay. If we need help finding someone else, can Ronan call you tomorrow? One of the cartel members left a couple of years before I did, and he's in Boston somewhere. We got his phone number tonight, but he hung up on me."

"Send it over. And anything you have on him. It might take me a while, but I'll find him." Wren yawns, then gasps. "Ry? Right there!" She points, and he moves his hand up, staring at Wren like she's the most beautiful woman he's ever seen.

"Holy fuck. That's her?" His eyes, mesmerizing with their multi-colored hues, are even more intense now, and the man actually smiles. "Later, Ronan. No one but Wren gets to hear me attempt baby talk."

Wren manages a quick "Bye" before the connection fades away, and I pull Zephyr into my arms. "We have help now, luv. Ryker McCabe doesn't back down. From anythin'. He doesn't joke either. When this is all over, you have a job waitin' for you if you want it."

"I don't know what to say. Why would any of you risk your lives...for me?" she asks.

"Because that's what we do."

<hr>

DANTE EMAILS me while Zephyr's brushing her teeth.

Got you some answers. Zephyr is 5'5" tall, thirty-four years old, and has green eyes. Approximate weight: 130 pounds. From the interviews I conducted, she appears to be claustrophobic, but her main weakness is family. She considers the Strauss Cartel her family and will do anything to protect them.

Rolling over, I snort into my pillow. The Strauss Cartel isn't Zephyr's family anymore. She's told me more than once that she loves her brother, but she knows he'd kill her without a second thought.

But the rest of it? Dante is absolutely in contact with someone in the cartel, and now we have proof. I send a quick text to Wren before setting my phone to emergency contacts only for the night. Anyone at Second Sight or Hidden Agenda will be able to get through to me, but that's it. The water in the bathroom shuts off, and I turn the phone face down on the nightstand. I don't want to trigger Zephyr any more tonight. We can talk about this in the morning.

When the woman I'm quickly falling for slips through the door, I can't tear my gaze away.

"One of these days, maybe I won't have to steal your t-shirts," she says, her voice soft, a hint of regret to her tone. "Some of the clothes I ordered should show up tomorrow."

"I love seein' you in my clothes. Borrow whatever you want. For as long as you want."

Zephyr shoots me a sideways glance as she slips under the covers, and the light hits her in such a way, the bruises from Theo's attack appear even worse than they did an hour ago.

"How's yer neck?" I trace the fingertip marks with a knuckle, and Zephyr sighs.

"Better than the rest of me. It's been a while since someone tackled me and threw me into a couple of walls."

"Shit. The bystander only captured the last part of the fight. I'm sorry I couldn't protect you, luv."

"You don't have to protect me," she says with a weak smile. "I can protect myself. Most of the time, anyway. I did make Theo scream like a baby after all."

Laughing, I wrap my arms around Zephyr. She fits so perfectly against me. Slight curves, taut muscles, and that silky, soft hair tickling my neck.

"Are all of your coworkers as intense as Ryker?" she asks.

"No. Or...not quite. Dax is a close second. He served with Ryker and Ripper. When you meet Dax, you might not realize it, but he's blind. Mostly. Can see some shadows and muted colors. Trevor was a CIA sniper. Ford was in the Marines. He's the oldest, and his wife always says he's a big teddy bear—as long as no one pisses him off. Clive is easy going. Ella...she keeps to herself. Tank...his nickname fits. He's a wall of muscle, but one of the nicest guys you will ever meet."

The more I talk about the men and women I work with, the more I realize how much they mean to me. And how relieved I am that Wren and Ry know about Zephyr. She's fast becoming my everything, and though the idea of telling Dax I lied—even by omission—scares the fuck out of me, I need him to know how I feel about her. I need everyone to know. Zephyr most of all.

CHAPTER TWENTY

Ronan

I REACH FOR THE LIGHT, but Zephyr stops me, her hand on my arm. "What are you doing? I distinctly remember telling you I wanted you naked tonight."

"You're exhausted, luv. You can have me naked any time you want, but I won't be hurtin' you."

She straddles me, her hands flat on my chest. "You won't hurt me." A hint of fear creeps into her eyes. "We don't know what's going to happen tomorrow, Ronan. I know you believe in your boss. In all of your coworkers, but Oliver, Theo, and probably François and Alex are somewhere in Boston. I lost everything four years ago. My identity, my freedom—my *life*. Yes, I've been alive, but I haven't been *living*. No more wasting time. The other night, you asked me to trust you for one moment. I did. But I was convinced that would be the *only* moment I let my guard down."

"Zephyr—" I can't put a name to the emotion churning in her eyes, but I ache to comfort her.

"No. Let me get this out. Please?" She dips her head for a

brief, soft kiss before she continues. "Every time I wanted to run, I heard your voice in my head, and I'd add one more moment. I have them all strung together now. But they aren't enough. I want more. And I want these moments we have together to *matter*."

Threading my fingers through her hair, I pull her down to claim her lips. The little moan she makes has me growing harder by the second, and by God, I need her like I need oxygen.

"You don't know what you do to me, luv," I manage when I break off the kiss.

Zephyr laughs, the sound so light and happy. "Oh, I think I have some idea." Sitting up, she peels off the t-shirt. Her shoulder is several shades of purple and blue, but the movement doesn't seem to pain her much.

With an arm around her back, I guide her lower until I can take one of the rosy, hard nubs into my mouth. Laving my tongue over and around her nipple, I relish each shiver, the way goosebumps race down her back, the scent of her arousal and her heat pressing to my aching dick.

She swivels her hips, and fuck. I didn't think I could want her more.

Reaching between us, I find the bottom edge of her panties and dip my finger under the cotton.

"You're so wet, luv. I need you naked and on your back. Right now."

Her smile is everything, and when she rolls off the bed to shimmy out of her panties, I shed my boxers so there's nothing between us.

Unlike our first coupling, I know some of what she likes now, and position her so her legs are bent and spread wide. Tasting her is coming home, her moans, gasps, and whimpers my favorite sounds other than her laugh.

"I'm goin' to make ya come. Just like this," I murmur against her clit. With each stroke of my tongue, she flies higher, and her heels dig into the mattress on either side of me.

One arm wraps around her thigh, and with the other, I part her plump lower lips and plunge a finger deep inside her channel.

Zephyr practically comes off the bed on a cry. "Yes! More!"

Oh, she'll have more. Much more. this night is ours, and I'm not going to let it end until we're both fully sated and too exhausted to move.

Adding a second finger, I swivel them until I find her g-spot. She's close. Her stomach trembles, her muscles coiled, taut, ready to leap over the edge of the abyss.

She won't last much longer, so I move my tongue faster and harder, swirling it around her clit, scoring my teeth gently over her most sensitive spot, and pumping my fingers in and out of her in time. She's beyond words now and grabs my forearm, squeezing hard.

I groan as more of her essence floods me, and the added vibration sends her flying. Her back arches, and her inner walls squeeze my fingers again and again. I'll never get enough of her. She might just be my forever.

For several minutes, I hold her under the covers, letting her tremors subside. She gives me a weak smile, her half-lidded eyes unfocused. "We're not done."

"No, we're not. Unless you want to be."

"Hell, no." With a shake of her head, her gaze clears. Reaching under the blankets, she finds my dick with gentle fingers, stroking the shaft slowly all the way to my crown.

"God, luv. I didn't know how much I wanted ya to touch me like that."

"Like this?" Again, she slides her hand up and down my

length, then circles her thumb around the head until I'm weeping for her. "I'm at a disadvantage," Zephyr purrs. "You've tasted me…"

Bringing her hand to her lips, she pops her thumb into her mouth and moans, her eyes locked on mine.

This has to be the hottest fucking thing I've ever seen. Until she wriggles lower, trailing kisses along my jaw, to my neck, over the tattoo on my chest, and all the way to the wiry patch of trimmed hair surrounding my dick.

"Someone manscapes."

"A bit. If you don't—"

"Oh, I'm a fan. But you had me at the first cup of tea, Ronan." Her gaze softens, and she smiles up at me. "Nothing you could ever do or not do to your body will change how I feel about you."

We're dancing perilously close to saying words I never thought I'd say. Words Zephyr gave up on a long time ago. I want to stop her, to pull her into my arms and ask her if she's as close to falling as I am. But she wraps her hand around the base of my shaft and takes me into her mouth, and I'm gone.

Hollowing out her cheeks, she sucks me, her tongue adding gentle pressure as she bobs up and down. With her free hand, she curls her fingers around my balls, and fuck me. It's so much. Almost too much.

"Won't…last…like this…" I whisper, and she firms her lips, pulling back with agonizing slowness until my crown pops free.

"You don't have to." Like an animal on the prowl, she crawls back up to join me. Her mouth seals over mine, mixing our tastes. And I didn't think anything could be hotter.

I was an idiot.

Blindly, I fumble for the bedside table drawer until my fingers close around a condom. Her tongue battles with mine, asserting her dominance as easily as she acquiesced to me just minutes ago. We're so perfectly matched, it scares me, but I wouldn't change a thing.

When I'm sheathed, she straddles me, bracing her hands on the headboard and lowering herself onto my hard length. "Is this okay?" she asks. "I don't mind being on the bottom…"

"Don't you dare worry. I think I'd like you in any position you could think of."

Wrapping my hands around her hips, I let her set the rhythm, then join in, rising to meet her thrust for thrust. She moves one hand to my uninjured shoulder, strengthening our connection, and damn if she doesn't clench her inner walls around me with every stroke.

"Don't look away. I want to see yer eyes until the last possible moment." I'm so close, I'll be lucky to last another minute, so I slide a hand between us and find her clit. The first gentle touch makes her whimper. The second sends a spasm rolling through her entire body.

Time slows, and my heart beat roars in my ears. She's my everything. My whole world. And when I lose control, she joins me, two people once drifting and alone, who've found a home together.

CHAPTER TWENTY-ONE

Zephyr

Loud buzzing rouses me from the best dream. Ronan and I were curled up on his couch under a blanket, watching the snow fall on Christmas Eve. Multi-colored lights on the tree —*our* tree—twinkled in the corner, and he leaned in, his lips tickling my ear, and said he loved me.

It was so very real, that when I open my eyes and realize my phone is making that annoying sound, tears threaten. I *want* that life. At least the chance for it. But until we can take the cartel down, I'll never have it.

The number on screen shocks me fully awake. "It's Martín," I hiss, and Ronan rolls over with a grunt, then sits up straight as I answer the call.

"What's the code word?" I ask before he has a chance to say anything.

"Peonies."

"Martín. Thank God. I've been trying to track you down for years." Leaning close to Ronan so he can hear both sides of the conversation, I hold my breath at the silence on the other end of the call. "Say something. Please."

"You're certain there's a team in Boston?" His voice holds none of the strength and command I remember, even though I'd recognize it anywhere.

"I had a run-in with Theo yesterday. They knew about your account at Boston National and bluffed their way into getting your PO Box address. But they don't know anything else. Yet. I only found your number by hacking into the bank's computer system. It was in a notes field completely separate from the address."

"*Merde!* I cannot stay here. In Boston. In this house. The risk is too great. I taught you not to trust anyone, Zephyr. And yet you have people you believe can help? How can I be certain they are not lying to you?"

"You taught me a lot of things, *mon professeur*. Including how to read people. Ronan was sent to bring me in, but he knows how to read people too, and he believed I was innocent. We have proof I was in Stockholm the day Jasper Yoden was murdered. His team found it last night, and they're going to clear my name."

The sound of a door closing, a zipper, and rustling carry over the line. "You are correct that I have evidence of many of the cartel's crimes. I was never as accomplished with technology as you were, *mon cher ami*. It is on a thumb drive I keep with me always. I am too old and too tired for this fight. But I will give it to you before I disappear."

"You don't have to run," I say, forcing each word over the desperation clogging my throat. "Tell me where to meet you. I'll bring Ronan, and we'll take you somewhere you'll be safe until this is all over with. Then you can have your life back. All of it. Go back to France if you want. Or anywhere. Without fear."

"No," he says sharply, then sighs. "This should have been my fight years ago, Zephyr. If I had been braver, I could have saved you much pain. But I am an old man now. A heart attack almost killed me not long after I left Madrid. I never fully recovered. Then my wife...she passed six months ago, and I have suffered two more attacks since that day. I will be with her soon, and then I will find peace. Until then, I will disappear."

"Martín..." I want to cry. To rage. To make François, Alex, all of them pay for stealing the lives of so many. "I have to see you one last time. Please."

"I will text you my address when I have finished packing. Meet me here, and I will give you the evidence I have. I only ask one thing in return," he says softly.

"Anything."

Ronan drapes his arm around my shoulders, offering quiet comfort and strength without a word.

"You will not follow me or try to change my mind. I want you to be free, Zephyr. *Mon cher*. But I cannot be a part of your fight."

It takes everything I have not to burst into tears, knowing I'm going to lose him minutes after I see him again. But I agree to his terms, and when he hangs up the phone, I collapse against Ronan's strong chest, my eyes dry, but my heart in a million pieces.

WITH EVERY HOUR THAT PASSES, my anxiety grows until my hands are shaking. Ronan sharing Dante's email message from the previous night helped slightly. One more piece of evidence against him. But until I see Martín, I won't be able to settle.

"Ya have to eat somethin', luv. Toast?" he asks, setting yet another cup of tea in front of me. I've had so much caffeine, I'm buzzing.

"What's taking him so long?" I ask.

"He's leavin' everythin' he has in the world." Sinking down

next to me, Ronan rubs gentle circles over my back. "That kind of packin' takes a little time. It's only been three hours. He said he had a wife. If she lived wherever he is now...that's got to be hard, yeah?"

Hearing Ronan put it like that, I kick myself for not being more understanding. Everything we have to do once we leave Ronan's apartment today? Say goodbye to Martín, get his evidence, go to Second Sight? It all weighs on me.

I should be happy. This amazing, handsome, protective man cares for me. Might even love me. But I'm too tense to tell him how I feel. Too on edge. Because if I say the words and he doesn't? I don't know what I'll do.

After he insists another half dozen times, I force down a few bites of toast. If nothing else, I need something to steady my hands. I've memorized Wren's cloud storage address and passkey, and once we get to Second Sight, I'll transfer all the files I have on the cartel to her—along with whatever I get from Martín.

My laptop—and only my laptop—is nestled in my backpack. I thought about packing all of my things. Even started. But Ronan believes so passionately that everything will work out today, I have to believe too.

"Finally!" I snatch my phone from the table before it stops buzzing to find an address on the screen. "How far away is this?"

Ronan pulls on his shoulder harness and tucks his Glock into the holster, then glances at the address. "Twenty minutes. Maybe thirty dependin' on traffic. Parts of Boston are a mess even when it's not rush hour. But I know a couple of shortcuts."

I tap out a quick reply telling Martín we're on our way and that we'll see him in under half an hour, slip on my shoes, and yet another pair of cheap, drugstore sunglasses. I don't bother to hide my hair. We'll be at Second Sight in less than two hours, and after that—I hope—I'll never have to run again.

RONAN WASN'T KIDDING about the traffic. Even with truly impressive defensive driving skills, it's a full twenty-eight minutes from his parking garage to Martín's house. We're not that far from the run-down neighborhood we visited yesterday.

Easing his car into an open space a little over a block away, Ronan turns to me, his blue eyes blazing with an intensity I can't ignore. "Stay by my side the whole time. I don't want a repeat of yesterday."

My fingers flutter over the bruises on my neck. One of the few times I wish I wore makeup. I didn't have anything to cover them with this morning. "Neither do I. But Martín might not trust you. Hang back just a few steps when I knock on his door."

He shakes his head. "Not happenin'."

"One step? My face has to be the first one he sees. Or he won't let us in at all. He'll be out the back in under ten seconds and we'll never see him again."

Whatever Ronan finds in my eyes or hears in my voice convinces him, because he nods, though from his scowl, he doesn't like it. "Fine. Let's go. The faster we can get to Second Sight, the better."

The house is as nondescript as they come in Boston. White paint, gray trim. Spider webs cover the light next to the door. Motioning to Ronan to stay at the bottom of the two wooden steps, I ring the doorbell.

For several seconds, nothing happens, but as I'm about to press the button again, two separate locks *thunk* and Martín stands in front of me.

His lined face holds nothing but sadness, and his hair—once black as night—is mostly gone on top, a yellowish gray on the sides. "Zephyr. My God. You...I never thought I would see you again."

The weariness in his voice tugs at my heart, and I gesture behind me. "This is Ronan. Can we come in?"

Martín shakes his head. "No. Only you."

"Over my dead body," Ronan growls.

"I will only speak to Zephyr." Martín stands up a little straighter, some of the fight back in his eyes.

"I won't be long," I say, turning to Ronan and linking our fingers. "You can wait right here. Martín won't hurt me."

"We agreed to stick together, luv." He touches his forehead to mine, and I can *feel* how much he wants—and needs—to protect me. The light from Martín's living room spills onto the top step, and I cast a quick glance inside. A small suitcase stands by a potted plant, but the rest of the room—what I can see of it, anyway—is in pristine order.

"Five minutes," I whisper. "You'll hear me if I need you."

"Five minutes. Not a second longer." He cups the back of my neck and pulls me in for a swift, hard kiss that sends shivers all the way to my toes. Before he releases my hands, he glares at Martín. "If you hurt her, I'll kill you myself."

Martín doesn't respond other than to step back and stare at his shoes. Adjusting my backpack on my shoulder, I follow him inside.

As soon as the door closes, Martín turns away. His shoulders shake, and I rush over to him. "I'm sorry I didn't find you sooner. I wanted to." As I'm about to touch his arm, someone grabs me from behind, a gloved hand clamping over my mouth and nose.

I can't call for Ronan. Can't breathe at all, and my heart hammers so hard, it feels like it's going to burst right out of my chest.

"Scream, shout, or make a single sound louder than a whisper, and Oliver will shred lover boy right through the door," Theo growls in my ear. He spins me around, and Oliver steps out from behind a wall, an M4 rifle aimed at the front door. "Nod if you understand."

I jerk my head down once—all the movement I'm capable of with my chest burning from lack of oxygen. Theo's hands fall away, and I whirl around, sucking in a deep breath and desperately trying to think of some way out of this.

"I'm so sorry, Zephyr," Martín says, sinking down to his knees. "They showed up as I was about to send you my address."

"Why didn't you warn me?" I hiss.

Martín's eyes water, and Theo pulls out a silenced pistol and presses it to the back of the old man's neck. "They promised it would be quick. And painless. I'll see my Laura again."

The quiet pop makes me jump, and Martín falls, almost in slow motion. Dropping my backpack and kneeling next to him, I cup his cheek. "No. Please, no." Blood seeps from the wound, so much less than I imagined, and he's so still.

Tears spill down my cheeks. I'm next. And Ronan? They have no reason to leave him alive. I have to find a way to warn him that doesn't end with my brother killing him.

Theo jabs my forehead with the still-warm silencer. "You have one chance to save the asshole outside the door," he says. "Come quietly, and he can live. We don't *want* a shootout in the middle of the day. But if you don't cooperate, we're prepared for one."

Her main weakness is family

Dante was right. I know what will happen to me if I let Theo and Oliver take me. I'll end up in a small, dark place until they're ready to break me. Until François exacts his revenge for every imagined wrong, for my *disloyalty*, for all the trouble I've caused the cartel over the last four years. But my fear of what they'll do to me? It's nothing compared to the pain I'll feel if they kill Ronan.

"We all leave together," I say quietly. "Through the back

door. Oliver first so I know he's not waiting behind to kill Ronan anyway. You put a single hand on me before we're at least a block away from here, and I'll scream so loud and long, the cops will hear it two states over."

I'm still on my knees, my hands clasped in my lap, and I slide my father's ring off my thumb. I need to know Ronan will have something of me when I'm gone.

"Deal. Now get up."

Bracing my hands on the floor, I lean down and kiss Martín's cheek. "I hope you're at peace, my old friend. I forgive you." The ring tucks just under his arm, and I get to my feet.

"Put these on." Theo holds out a pair of flexi-cuffs, and I barely resist the urge to roll my eyes.

"You going to walk me down the street in these and expect no one will notice?"

Shoving his gun into a shoulder harness under his jacket, he snorts. "Of course not. You're going to pick up that coat on the back of the couch and use it to hide the cuffs. Quit being a smartass or our deal's off."

I have to use my teeth to tighten the second cuff and try to give myself a little bit of slack, but Theo checks them before he gives the order to move and tightens them to the point I'm scared I'll lose all feeling in my hands before we make it to their vehicle.

With the coat draped over my wrists, I follow Oliver out the kitchen door, Theo right on my heels, my backpack slung over his shoulder.

Snow falls steadily, and my cheeks prickle with the cold. Has it been five minutes yet? Has Ronan knocked? Burst in? Found Martín's body?

No one says a word—or stops—until we're just over a block from Martín's house next to an older model black sedan. Theo pops the trunk, and I try to back away. "No. Not in there. I'll go anywhere you want. I won't put up a fight. But don't put me in there."

"Relax, bitch," he says, pulling a small, zippered pouch from his jacket pocket. "You won't be awake long enough to care."

Oliver slings an arm around my shoulders, looking to anyone watching like he's the friendliest guy in the world, but his grip is tight enough to hurt, and he has me wedged against the back of the car with Theo right in front of me.

The syringe glints in the streetlights, and my whole body shakes. "No. Not like this. Oliver, please. We're family. Don't you remember the years...before?"

Theo jabs the needle into my neck and presses down on the plunger. I want to scream, but terror has me frozen, my heart racing. What did he give me? How long will it take?

"We're not family," Oliver says sharply. "We stopped being family the day you got Jessica killed."

Theo glances around, then turns back to me and grins. At least, I think he does. Everything's softer now. Dimmer. His voice sounds different too. Slower. Deeper. "Time to go, street rat. Next stop? A world of pain."

Falling. Acrid smells. Something hard against my back. A swath of light getting smaller, then a loud bang. Then nothing at all.

CHAPTER TWENTY-TWO

Ronan

WHAT THE FUCK is taking so long? I gave Zephyr five minutes. Then another three. The old man isn't a threat to her, and he opened the door wide enough for me to see the whole living room. Sparse. But with a handful of feminine touches. A lace slipcover over the couch. Pictures on a bookcase. A single painting of a beach sunset on the far wall.

At nine minutes on the dot, I'm past caring if Zephyr's mad at me for interrupting her reunion with her friend.

Two steps inside, I catch my first whiff of blood. My world grinds to a halt. Zephyr's gone. Martín's body lies on the floor, his eyes open and staring, a small pool of blood behind his head.

Drawing my gun, I force myself to clear the entire house, even though it's painfully obvious Zephyr isn't here. The back door is unlocked, and I check the alley, running to one end, then the other, but she's gone.

How could I have been so stupid?

Because you're in love with her. Because she wasn't worried. Because you wanted her to have this final moment with Martín.

Returning to the house, I kneel next to the body and close the old man's eyes. A glint of silver draws my gaze. Zephyr's ring. It's tucked halfway under Martín's arm, somewhere it wouldn't have landed accidentally. She left it for me.

Sliding it onto my pinky, I get to my feet, take a quick video of the scene, set the back deadbolt and exit the way I came in, depressing the button on the front door handle so it locks behind me.

As soon as I start my car, I connect my phone to the hands-free. "Call Dax."

"Ronan, you better be on your way here with Zephyr," he says the moment he answers.

"The cartel has her." Saying the words destroys me, but I have to hold it together if I have any hope of finding her alive. "I need...fuck. They took her...and I was twenty feet away. I should have *known*. Done somethin'."

"Stop." His order echoes through the car. "Where are you right now?"

Jabbing the button on my dashboard that activates my GPS unit, I gun the engine to make it through a traffic light before it turns red. "Ten minutes from Second Sight."

"Get here. Where was she taken from? I'll call Wren and have her start hacking the cameras in the area."

My voice cracks as I give him Martín's address. They haven't had her long enough to seriously hurt her. Yet. But they will. Shit. Dax is saying something.

"...if you get into a wreck, you'll be no use finding her. Do you understand me?"

"Yeah. Don't die. Got it."

THE OFFICE IS ALMOST COMPLETELY quiet when I enter. What the fuck?

Marjorie hurries down the hall toward me. "Everyone's in the conference room. They're all waiting for you, and food is on the way."

"Food?" Eating is the last thing I care about. Images flash through my mind on a loop. Zephyr's face twisted in pain. Theo using God-knows-what to whip her back, torturing her with a car battery, locking her in a small, dark box where she can't breathe, can't think, can't escape.

Taking my arm and jerking me back to the present, Marjorie leads me to Second Sight's main conference room. "If you don't eat, you won't be able to think, hon. *This* is why I'm here. I'm not one to fight. Or hack. I don't have friends in governments all over the world or any tactical experience. That's your specialty. It's my job to take care of everyone. You go in there and do your job. I'll do mine."

She opens the door to chaos. A large video screen with Wren in the top left and a street view of Martín's house in the top right draws my attention until Trevor looks up from his seat next to Tank. "Ronan. Are you hurt? Did the cartel—"

"They didn't touch me. Hell, I never saw them. But Martín Levi—he left the cartel before Zephyr did—is dead. Someone shot him once in the back of the head. Whoever did it used a silencer, because I didn't hear a fuckin' thing."

Dax rises, bracing his hands on the conference table. "I'm goin' to ask you this once. Are you sure Zephyr didn't kill him?"

I have my boss pinned to the wall—rage stealing what little rational thought I had left—before I even register I've moved. "They *took her*! Zephyr wouldn't have left me, and she sure as shit wouldn't have shot a sixty-five-year-old man in the back of the head!"

Dax doesn't kick my ass. Doesn't try to dislodge my hands

from his shoulders. But the way his gaze bores into mine from behind the glasses? I swear he can see me. "Are you done?"

"Done?"

He's so calm, it would be terrifying if I cared one bit about my own life right now. "Yes, done. If so, answer the goddamned question and get your hands off me."

"Dax, leave the kid alone." The rough voice booming from the speakers surprises everyone, and I release my boss to see Ryker standing behind Wren on screen. "Ronan's right. Zephyr wouldn't have left him. And she's not a killer. We have proof of that."

"Care to tell me where this proof came from? And how the hell would you know what she would or wouldn't do?" Dax takes a tentative step forward until his right hand brushes the edge of the conference table.

"Wren found a photo of Zephyr in Stockholm on the day Yoden was killed," Ryker says. "As for the latter? She loves him. We saw that plain as day last night."

Dax turns in my direction. "*Love? Last night*? You said you'd talked to her. You never told me you were *sleeping* with her."

"Because all you wanted to do was turn her over to the authorities! Every fuckin' time I tried to tell you she was innocent, that this case was a mess, you told me I had a job to do, and you expected me to do it!"

Removing his glasses, Dax sinks down into his chair and pinches the bridge of his nose. It's his go-to move when he's thinking or frustrated. "Yes. I expected you to do your job. Do you remember what your job *was*? Bring in Jasper Yoden's killer. You told me Zephyr didn't kill him, but you were being so goddamned cagey, I didn't know what the hell was going on. I should have called you on it. And I should have listened."

He rises and, in two steps, he's standing directly in front of me, anguish written in the lines around his eyes, the set of his jaw. "I'm sorry, Ronan."

I'm so shocked at the apology, I can't form a response. Until Dax pounds the table hard enough to rattle all the water glasses someone—probably Marjorie—set out for us. "We've wasted too much time not being *completely* honest with one another. That stops now. Understood?"

One by one, we all agree, and the video screen splits to show the street behind Martín's house. "I pulled this just a few minutes ago," Wren says.

Zephyr walks between Oliver and Theo, her hands clasped in front of her. The three of them turn right, walk another half a block, and stop next to a black sedan. Oliver pins Zephyr against the car, and she struggles until Theo reaches for her neck. Under a minute later, they toss her into the trunk, slam the lid, and drive away.

"Those two men are...fuck. I need a minute." Stalking over to the window, I stare out at the snow falling steadily. We're supposed to get six inches today. Even more tomorrow. And they threw her into the trunk of a car.

Behind me, Wren takes over and fills everyone in. "The man in front of Zephyr shares her basic bone structure. Pretty safe to say that's her brother, Oliver. Facial recognition is running on all the traffic cameras in the area and against all known databases, but as you know, that could take days to get a positive match. The other man is Theodore Hallswell. We know *a lot* about him. He's been arrested more than once. The last time was in Nice, France, for assault, false imprisonment, and manslaughter, but the case was dismissed after every credible witness disappeared or recanted their story."

"That's the cartel's doing. The last time they captured Zephyr," my voice cracks, and I brace my arm on the window, "Theo tortured her for three days. She barely survived." Shit. I can't do this. Can't talk about her pain *knowing* she's going to suffer so much more. Might already *be* suffering. Trevor takes my arm and guides me to a chair.

"Sit, man. Before you fall down."

Wren clears her throat. "Ronan, I followed the car for three miles before it entered a dead zone. All the traffic cameras in a six-block radius were disabled or jammed. They went offline at 10:00 a.m. this morning and came back online two minutes ago. The car never emerged from that black hole."

Dax turns to Second Sight's newest junior investigator. "Tank? I want you all over that area. Every parking garage. Alley. Side street. Let us know what you find."

"On it. Wren, send the map to my phone?" he asks.

"Already there."

"They'll take her somewhere private," Trevor says. "That neighborhood is densely populated. Ronan, tell us everything you know about the cartel's movements since Zephyr arrived in Boston. We need to find patterns. Run probabilities."

I drop my head into my hands. "And pray. Because we're goin' to need a miracle to save her."

Zephyr

It's dark. Cold. More than cold. Frigid. Everything hurts. My back. Arms. Legs. My head most of all. I can't raise it more than an inch. The sedative Theo gave me is keeping my panic *almost* manageable, but that won't last long. I'm stuffed in a rough, wooden box so small, my knees are forced up under my chin, and there's no light. No give to the slats.

Tugging at my wrists, I cry out as the cuffs cut into my skin. "Please," I whisper. "Whatever...you're going to do...get it over with."

I can't scream. Can't beg for my life. That's what they want. Theo. François. Even Oliver. But with every minute that passes, I'm more alert. My chest stutters, and I try to count. Breathe in for four. Hold for seven. Out for eight. But I can't even manage the first few seconds.

My body flails, no longer listening to my brain's desperate attempts to stay calm. Banging my head and shoulders against the wood, I can't feel the pain. Only the enormous weight of the panic attack pressing down on me. My heels scrape the bottom, and splinters dig into my soles. Splinters. Oh, my God. I'm not wearing shoes. Or socks. I can feel my bra. My panties. Nothing else.

They took my clothes.

So they can hurt me.

My world shrinks down to a single pinpoint of light coming from a crack in the wood. It's so small, I wonder if I'm imagining it. But it's all I have. The only thing that can stop me from going under.

They'll keep me in here for hours. Alone. Freezing. Until I can't stand another minute. Until I'm so frantic, so cold, so desperate to see daylight, I won't be able to stop myself from begging.

François won't listen. He won't care.

And then...there will be pain.

BRIGHT LIGHT SEARS MY EYES, and I squeeze them shut so I don't have to see what's coming. I'm so cold, the hands that yank me out of the box burn my skin.

"I hope you slept well, street rat," Theo says. "It'll be the last good rest you get for a very long time."

He drags me across a smooth floor, and when I open my eyes to slits, I see nothing but gray. Concrete. It's a huge space, given how Theo's voice echoed.

A hint of warmth bathes my frigid limbs, and I relish in it until it turns hot. Then my skin starts to burn.

Theo drops me, and I crumple in a heap on the floor that feels like liquid lava. Logically, I know it's not, but that doesn't make it hurt any less.

Whimpering, I try to stretch out my legs, but crippling, agonizing cramps put a stop to that. So many sensations hit me at once, I don't notice Theo cutting the flexi-cuffs until my arms flop forward and my shoulders cry out in pain.

"Get her up," he orders, and a shadow looms over me.

Robbie—one of François's minions—yanks me by the arm and throws me into a chair. I'm too weak to stand or fight, and Theo knows it. He and Robbie take their time, tying my wrists to the arms of the chair with thin cord. My ankles are bound together next, and I realize why it feels like I'm burning to death.

Heat lamps. They surround this small area.

"You can scream as much as you want," Theo says, stepping in front of one of the lights. Backlit, he looks like a Neanderthal. Then again, he looks like that on his best day. "And you *will* scream. We have put our lives on hold for you so many times over the past four years. Because you betrayed us. You stole from us."

"Fuck you. I *left* and François framed me for murder." My head is almost clear, but it does me no good tied to a chair. If no one cares if I scream, we must be in the middle of nowhere. Or in a neighborhood that's totally deserted. Boston doesn't have many of those.

Theo leans closer, and the syringe in his hand makes me squirm, but all I manage to do is rattle the chair. The needle pierces the skin of my elbow, and he grins as he depresses the plunger.

"The last time we were together, I did not know half of what I know now. For example, I can inject you with a mix of powerful stimulants, and not only will you feel *everything* I do to you on an even grander scale, but you will not be able to pass out from the pain."

My heart is already racing, and as the drug works its way through my body, my skin prickles, and it feels like my head's about to explode. "What...did you...give me?" I wheeze.

His laugh is completely at odds with the cold detachment in his eyes. "Do not worry about that. Worry about what comes next."

CHAPTER TWENTY-THREE

Zephyr

"Ready for more?" Theo taunts.

Robbie pries my thumb from its death grip on the arm of the chair.

The four other fingers of my left hand spasm uncontrollably, a needle protruding from under each nail.

"D-do...it," I rasp.

My heart races from the cocktail of stimulants, and even the gentlest touch feels like sandpaper on my skin. Under the heat lamps, my body burns, and I can't catch my breath. "I needed... a manicure."

Robbie frowns—he never was the smartest—and looks up at Theo, my thumb clenched in his fist so hard, he's about to snap the bone. "Are you sure this is painful?"

Theo cuffs him on the side of the head. "She's lying, idiot. Hold her still."

Fire sears the sensitive nerves under my thumbnail. The sound I make? It's not human. I won't scream. Can't give him the satisfaction. But soon, these keening whimpers and strangled groans won't be enough. For me or for him. Or François. He's watching. Somewhere close.

"Five down. Five to go. Then we start on your toes." Theo stands, brushing his hands together with a smug, self-satisfied grin.

Robbie passes him a bottle of water, and he breaks the seal, gulping half of it down while I writhe desperately against the ropes.

I can't take my eyes off the bottle. Hours under the lamps. Dripping with sweat.

"Oh, would you like some?" he asks, waving the bottle in front of my face.

"W-wouldn't...touch it. M-might catch s-something." I'd spit on him if my mouth weren't bone dry.

Robbie grabs my hair and wrenches my head back. Water splashes my face, blessedly cool, but I wasn't prepared. A single swallow is all I can capture. The rest rolls down my body, joining the large puddle of my sweat on the floor.

"Do you want to know how I *convinced* Martín to hand over his thumb drive?" Theo asks.

The memory of my friend, his eyes open, chest still, threatens to swallow me whole, and I shake my head, clamping my lips together so hard between my teeth, I taste blood.

Robbie flicks each one of the needles, chuckling. My vision goes white. The scream is muffled behind my lips but giving in to my own weakness is the worst kind of torture.

Coming up behind me, Theo whispers in my ear. "Like this." A knuckle digs into a pressure point between my shoulder and neck.

Everything stops. I can't breathe. Can't make a sound. My mouth is open, my muscles straining against the ropes. He lets up, but before I can do more than suck in a wheezing breath, moves to the other shoulder.

Dark streaks obscure my vision. I hear nothing but the rapid-fire beat of my heart. The pain fades away. Or do I?

A harsh odor burns my nose, and I jerk. The chair rattles.

"Can't have you passing out." Theo waves a small paper capsule—now broken—in front of my face. Smelling salts. "I can't give you another shot for at least forty-five minutes. And we have so much to do before then."

I no longer scream. I can't. After the third finger of my right hand, Robbie had to tie my torso to the back of the chair. I'm too weak to sit up.

Spots float in front of my eyes. Theo's face is fuzzy. Don't have to worry about seeing the needles anymore. Too small. Too far away. My toes...even the pressure of the concrete underneath them is too much.

No more. Kill me. Please.

"I have been looking for you for a long time, street rat," a smooth voice says as footsteps draw closer.

François.

Someone yanks my head up, and the man I hate most in this world grabs my chin. Thick fingers threaten to crush my jawbone. Thank God, I'm too weak to make a sound.

"I know you stole files from us before you left. I need them back. All of them."

Do my eyes convey what I'm screaming in my head?

"Fuck you."

"Not ready to talk?" He squeezes harder, and I whimper. "Maybe some time alone will help that."

My head falls forward. Every breath is a struggle. A small sting at my elbow barely registers until my fractured thoughts catch up with reality. The stimulants kick in, and I sit up straight, jerking my hands against the ropes. My eyes feel like they're bulging. Maybe they are.

Robbie and Theo each take one of my hands. Oh, fuck. The needles hurt more coming out than going in. Halfway through, one of them rouses me with a packet of smelling salts. They have to use another after finishing with my toes.

Blood oozes around my wrists. My heart pounds. But I'm too weak to fight. I watch, helpless, as they cut the ropes.

The floor rushes up to meet me. God. It's so hot.

Robbie wrenches my arms behind my back. More ropes, then I'm moving. Being dragged by my bound ankles.

Oh, God. Not the box. *Not the box.*

The concrete cools. Ice cold now. Cold can burn like fire. I forgot that. Or did I?

"N-no..." I moan when the two of them lower me into the crate.

Theo tips a fresh bottle of water to my lips, and I suck down two gulps before he pulls it away.

The lid forces my head down, and darkness presses in on me. Metal. A lock. Footfalls. Getting quieter. Then nothing. Silence.

My breaths come faster and faster. The pitch black around me spins. But I don't pass out. I can't. They've trapped me with my panic. No way out. No way through.

Ronan. I'm sorry.

I picture his face. The rough stubble. Recall his scent. Fresh rain. Clean and woodsy. But his voice...I can't remember his voice. Can't hear it. And I need it. So badly. Need...him.

Ronan

Snow falls steadily outside the conference room window. No one's gone home. Hell, even Marjorie is still here.

Tank found the car Theo and Oliver used in the corner of an underground parking garage. A few drops of blood led from the trunk to the adjacent parking space, which means they used a second car—one we can't possibly trace—to move her.

Ripper took over for Wren a little after 9:00 p.m. Ryker practically had to drag her away from the computer.

The door swings open, and I turn away from the window. West Sampson, former Navy SEAL and one of Ryker's team, takes one look around the room and shakes his head. "Ford? Get some sleep. You too, Clive. The probie will wake you in three hours."

Raelynn, her blond hair pulled into a tight ponytail, edges around the SEAL and dumps her pack in the corner of the room. She only started with Hidden Agenda a couple of months ago, but she helped rescue Quinton, Graham's guy, less than twenty-four hours after her initiation exercise. "The probie this, the probie that," she mutters. "When are we goin' to hire someone else, anyway?"

"When Ry says so." West's sharp reply shuts her up, and she claims a corner of the conference table for her laptop and phone. "Ronan, pick your jaw up off the floor. Did you really think we weren't going to come?"

"I..." The voice in my head won't shut up, and my shoulders slump. "I don't know what any of us are doin' here. She's gone, and the cartel is goin' to kill her."

Dax swivels his chair to face me. "If we gave up every time we ran into a brick wall, half of us wouldn't be alive right now."

He's right. Wren. Trevor. Joey. Ripper. Nodding, I reach for the water pitcher Marjorie fills at regular intervals. My hands shake, and West eases it from my grip. "You're taking a couple of hours too, Ronan. As soon as you tell us everything that's happened in the past few days. We've heard the second-hand accounts. We need yours."

"What good is that goin' to do?" I down the glass of water in four gulps, and West refills it, glaring at me.

"Maybe nothing. Maybe everything. No detail is too small where these fuckers are concerned. Names, descriptions, who's the muscle? The brains? Both? Fighting styles. It's all important."

In the upper corner of the video screen, a timer counts up. Zephyr's been gone for almost eight hours now.

"They had me for three days. They'd shove me into the storage trunk when they were done with every torture session. Seven, eight times, I think."

Three days. Seventy-two hours. Eight times in the trunk. If they kept a regular schedule, same time in the trunk as out of it...

Meeting West's gaze, I swallow hard. "Based on what Zephyr told me about the last time they captured her, they'll spend at least four or five hours torturin' her, then lock her in a small, dark space for the same amount of time. Even *tellin'* me about it left her shattered. She's one of the strongest people I've ever known, but these fuckers are twisted bastards who won't stop until they destroy her. And only after she's broken so thoroughly, there's nothin' left, will they let her die."

Understanding swims in the SEAL's eyes. His expression never changes, nor does his stance. But he nods. "Then let's get to work."

CHAPTER TWENTY-FOUR

Zephyr

MY CONSTANT SHIVERING slows to the occasional shudder. This is bad. My hands and feet are numb. I can't feel my nose. My lips.

Each wheezing breath forces my back against the wood. Splinters dig into my spine. They feel like toothpicks—or two-by-fours—and for once, I'm grateful for the pain. It's the only evidence I'm still alive.

"They promised it would be quick."

Martín's whispered words echo in the silence of the box.

Would François make me the same deal?

Can't last much longer.

"P-please," I call weakly. "Let...me out..."

So tired. So thirsty. My stomach twists into knots. My heart races, skips beats until I'm dizzy, then races again. Arrythmia is bad. Really bad.

"If I die in here...assholes, you'll...be next. François...wants his...files back."

Time has no meaning anymore, but I think only a few minutes pass before the lock snaps open, and light pours in.

"Fuck," Theo mutters. "Her lips are blue. Get her out of there."

I can't feel the hands on my arms this time. Or the leg cramps. Or much at all. Only those damn splinters.

Back in the chair. Tied down. Heat setting my frozen body on fire. Blinking hard, I struggle to focus on the table half a dozen feet away. Didn't see it last time. Scalpels. More needles. Syringes.

François picks up a length of rope, drawing it through his fingers. "Are you ready to tell me where we can find the files you stole?"

"Water..." I manage. My tongue barely works, and my lips are cracked and bloody.

"Not until you answer me." The rope flies, hitting me across the chest. It stings, but I'm still half-numb. "Dose her again," he snaps, and Theo picks up a syringe.

"No!" I sound like a dying frog, and the thought is so ridiculous, I want to laugh. Is this what it's like to lose your mind? I drift on that thought until the sting of the needle brings me back. "Can't...type if you drug me."

"Stop, Theodore." François's order comes too late, and the cocktail is already speeding through my bloodstream. Maybe... if I can focus long enough...I can convince them to kill me.

"Sorry, boss," Theo says.

François glares at him, but after a moment, shakes his head. "No matter. Bring her computer. Get Oliver, too."

Robbie hustles out of the ring of hot lights, and François saunters over to me, the rope doubled over so he can slap it against his palm.

"Please. I n-need...water." My gaze follows the rope. Up and down. Up and down. Each impact makes me flinch. I'm warming up now. My abused fingernails send sparks of pure agony racing through my fingers, and I don't know how the hell I'm going to be able to type.

François gestures for Theo to bring one of the bottles, but I only get a single sip before it's taken away. I strain against the ropes, a weak whimper escaping between my panting breaths as I try to follow it.

Footsteps. Another table slams down on the concrete floor, along with a chair. "Finally gave up, sis?" Oliver asks. "About damn time. Can't believe you lasted this long on your own."

"You're not alone anymore."

Ronan. I *didn't* forget his voice. The memory makes my eyes burn, but I'm too dehydrated to cry. I can almost *feel* him holding my hand as we talked to his friends.

Wren.

Her secure storage can log my location. Ronan will be looking for me. Assuming Oliver didn't double back. And if he did...someone would have found his body by now. His boss would tell Wren. Wren would explain everything.

Maybe.

It's such a long shot...but it's the only one I have.

The laptop boots up, and François leans down so we're face to face. "Tell your brother what to do, and maybe we won't have to break *every* bone in your body before the end."

Wren's storage is empty. Once they see that, they'll hurt me. Worse than they've ever hurt me before. But maybe there will still be something left of me to save if Ronan gets here in time.

"It's a fingerprint scanner, boss," Oliver says, picking up the laptop and hustling over to me. François grabs my right index finger and bends it back to the point I'm shocked it doesn't dislocate. I swallow my scream, clenching my teeth until the computer unlocks and he releases me.

"You need...to connect...to the internet," I rasp. "The cell phone...icon."

"Duh." Oliver clicks around, and God…I hope there's a cell tower close by. "Now what?"

"Type this…into the browser…" Slowly, each number harder to say than the last, I give Oliver the address of Wren's storage server.

"Passphrase?" my brother asks.

I'm so tired. Everything hurts. Can't focus. Until François lets the rope fly against my cheek with so much force, my entire head jerks.

"Yellow. Alpha. Dictionary. Fortune. Trainer. Light. Peacock. Heart. Carry. Ring."

Please work. Please find me.

"Uh, François?" Oliver frowns. This isn't going to end well for me. "There's nothing here."

"What?" He stalks over to the laptop and stares at the screen. "You little bitch."

"Everything…should be there." I try to act surprised, but I doubt he believes me. I wouldn't. "Try again."

Oliver returns his hands to the keyboard, but François grabs one of the scalpels, spins my brother's chair around, and presses the sharp blade to Oliver's neck. "Tell me where the files *really* are, or I will end him!"

"No!" I cry. "Don't hurt him!" My brother stopped being my family years ago. But I can't let François kill anyone but me.

"Where are they?" he shouts. "Give me everything. Right fucking now!"

Oliver wraps his hands around François's wrist, and the two struggle for control as I beg them to stop.

"I'll tell you! Everything!" But just as I give up all hope of keeping the files hidden, Oliver loses his grip on François's arm. Momentum drives the scalpel across his throat.

Blood sprays my laptop. Paints Oliver's gray t-shirt crimson. He gurgles and presses his hands to his neck. His eyes roll back in his head. And then he's gone.

"*You* did this," François roars.

I'm sobbing now, though my body is too far gone for tears. "No. You did. Break every bone. I don't fucking care. I'll never give you *anything*."

His rage boils over, and he tells tell Theo to do his worst.

Please, Ronan. Hurry. Or there won't be anything left of me to find.

Ronan

A rough shake pulls me from a nightmare. Zephyr's broken, bloodied body lay in the middle of a field, riddled with bullets. I'd pulled her into my arms, only to find her still warm. Minutes too late.

"Get up," Trevor says. "She's alive."

I'm on my feet in a heartbeat, almost knocking the former CIA sniper on his ass in my cramped office. "How do you know?"

"She accessed some internet site Wren set up? I didn't understand half of what Ripper said, but it logged an approximate location for her out past Randolph."

"That's over an hour away! How long ago did this happen?"

Following Trevor back to the conference room, my heart sinks when he answers. "Twenty minutes ago."

"Jesus, Mary, and Joseph. How come it took you so long to come get me?"

On the video screen, Ripper raises his head, anguish written all over his face. "I was deep in the traffic camera logs, trying to trace the hack that shut them down. The alert was on my second monitor. I fucked up, Ronan. If we're too late...it's because of me."

"No," Dax snaps. "You will *not* take the blame for this. You were doin' what I asked, and the second you saw the alert, you were on it."

The two of them might be closer than brothers, but Ripper doesn't give a fuck what Dax is saying.

I step right in front of the webcam so there's no way Rip won't see my eyes. "Dax is right. How were you supposed to know these assholes would let her within a thousand feet of a computer?"

"We lost *twenty minutes*," Rip says. "There's nothing on that file share."

The man is close to shutting down. To falling into his own memories from six years of brainwashing at the hands of a depraved Afghan megalomaniac who used to throw him into an old well and let dozens of scorpions sting him until he was crazed from the pain.

"Zephyr knows accessin' that share logs her location. She'll hold on as long as she can. But we need to stop kickin' ourselves and figure out exactly where she is." With every word, I try to believe. But from what she told me about François, he's not one to forgive, or give her a second chance once she fails to give him what he wants.

West clicks a remote control and a mirror of his tablet pops up next to Ripper on screen. "This is a map of the area within a five-mile radius of the cell tower the ping came from. It's nothing but industrial parks and open fields. This complex," he circles a grouping of six buildings, "is our best bet. But every single structure is empty. They could be in any of them. Rip is pulling blueprints now, and we'll need a separate infil plan for each of them."

"Fuck. How long is that goin' to take?"

"As long as it needs to," the SEAL snaps. Almost immediately, he shakes his head. "Sorry. I know what's at stake here, Ronan. But near as we can tell, there are at least five members of the cartel in Boston. Including the leader, François Strauss.

Dax and Austin have been working the phones all night, and every one of them has multiple suspected kills. If we rush this without a plan, we could all end up dead."

He's right. I know he's right, but that doesn't help when the only images running through my head are from my nightmare. "What can I do?" Infil isn't my bag. Surveillance, weapons, hell, even hand-to-hand combat. But I'm not a strategy guy like West is.

"Take Raelynn to your equipment room and help her load everything we'll need. There's a bird due on the roof in twenty minutes to fly us to a field eight miles from the complex. Any closer, and they'll hear us coming. There will be a van waiting for us when we land. We go in fast and get out quick, and take as many of those fuckers out as we can, but our top priority is Zephyr."

Raelynn stands and stretches, her back popping loudly. "Well, come on, Ronan. Show me where y'all keep the cool toys."

CHAPTER TWENTY-FIVE

Zephyr

"Load the box onto the truck," François says. "We'll dump it in the reservoir. She can drown. Screaming. And pack up all our equipment. I want to be out of here in twenty minutes."

Hunched over inside the cold, dark space, blood streaming from dozens of cuts, fresh electrical burns on my stomach, and so weak, they didn't even bother to bind my wrists this time, I rest my forehead on my knees.

Twenty minutes. That's all I have left.

I wish I could have seen Ronan one more time. Told him I love him. That I was stupid for not giving him all the evidence I had.

Something bangs into the box—hard—and I yelp. A strange sound—a rhythmic light thumping—accompanies my entire world shaking. Then I'm moving. Some sort of forklift?

It feels like forever before we stop again, and whoever's in charge of this thing obviously needs lessons, because the box shakes as it slams into something metallic, and a crack of light appears to my left.

Rising again, those same thumps, and then I hear Robbie's laugh a second before the box tips over.

My knees hit, along with my head. And the crack gets bigger. I can see through it now. Corrugated metal. A truck bed. Beyond that, lights spaced at regular intervals. Some sort of warehouse?

I count to a hundred, hoping that's enough time for Robbie to head back to wherever the rest of the crew is before I throw my entire body against the left wall.

Wood splinters. Not enough. So I try again. The impact is excruciating, and so loud, I'm certain someone's going to hear me. But I can stick my fingers through the opening.

They're so stiff, I struggle to bend them around the splintered wood. It's my only chance, and I will *not* let the pain stop me. The stimulants are wearing off, and I'm so tired, but I have to believe Ronan knows where I am. That he's on his way. That if I can get out of here and hide from François and his band of assholes, Ronan will find me.

"Come *on*," I grunt and try to twist my body in the cramped space. I need more leverage. It's impossible to get my feet against the left side, but I twist the other way, ignoring the dozens of fresh splinters until my back is pressed to the broken board and my feet to the opposite side.

This is going to be bad.

With all I have in me, I push with my legs. The gashes on my back tear open again, but a loud crack spurs me on, and after a few seconds' rest, I try again.

Two more boards pop free, and I'm staring up at the ceiling, my head, shoulders, and one arm free. That's all I need.

That and the strength to stand.

Opting to crawl first, I creep to the edge of the truck bed and pull myself up.

Please don't let anyone see me.

Voices come from somewhere deep in the warehouse. Too

far away to make out what they're saying. I have to move. Have to get out of the truck and find a closet, a vent shaft, a door...

The ground is so far away. But Robbie didn't close the tailgate, so I scoot to the edge, dangle my feet over the side, and let myself fall.

Ronan

West aims a thermal imaging gun at the third building in the massive complex. The first two were empty. Cold. This one is the largest. A storage facility for farm equipment, up until three years ago, it's been vacant ever since.

"Bingo," he says, his voice so quiet if the bone-conduction mics weren't the most sensitive in the world, I never would have heard him. "Grouping of heat signatures on the second level. Offices up there, from the blueprints. Can't get a read on the back of the place from this angle."

The plan he came up with for this building? Flashbangs if the assholes were close to a door. Silent infil and ambush if they weren't.

"Tank. You and Probie take the rear. Trevor, Ronan, and I are going in the front. Unless you encounter a goddamn white flag and the fucker waving it drops flat in under three seconds, we are *not* taking prisoners. Understood?"

One by one, everyone confirms the orders. No one who touched Zephyr gets to walk out of here. Especially not François Strauss.

West takes the lead, keeping to the shadows until the last possible second. A glass-walled reception area is dark, but next to it on the building's outer wall, is a metal door. West shoulders his M4, drops to one knee, and has the lock picked in under a minute. Signaling his orders, he yanks open the door.

Trev corners to the left, leaving me to clear the right. West follows, and we creep along the wall until we can see the offices.

"Target O is down," Tank says over comms. "Throat cut. Couple of hours ago. Broken laptop keys on the ground, and a fuckton of blood in two spots. This is where they had the package, but she's not here."

No. God, no.

Trevor rests his hand on my shoulder and squeezes once. Tank didn't say he found her body. Just Oliver. There's a chance she's still alive.

Gunfire explodes toward the back of the warehouse, and we all tense.

"Pinned down behind a stack of pallets," Raelynn says. "Two shooters. We'll keep 'em busy."

West signals for Trevor to head their way, then points at the stairs down from the offices. Two men, François and Alex Strauss, are already at the bottom and moving quickly to the south side of the building.

Where the fuck is Zephyr?

Waving his hand in front of my face, West glares at me. "Move your ass," he whispers. "We need one of them alive until we find the package."

More gunfire, then Trevor's voice. "One hostile down."

We're within a hundred feet of the Strauss brothers when François lobs something back over his shoulder.

"Cover!" West shouts, and I dive behind a pillar while the SEAL grabs a fucking grenade and throws it toward the door. The roar is deafening, and the front wall of the structure collapses in a heap of cement and twisted metal.

West is face down, and I rush over to him, checking for a pulse until he groans. "Fuck."

A shot hits the concrete a foot away, sending fragments pelting us. The two brothers stand side by side, each of them with a gun aimed at our heads. "Which one of you is the lover boy?" François asks. "She screamed for you. Many times. Until I broke her."

I start to lunge for him, but a bullet flies just over my shoulder, and West grabs my vest and yanks me back down.

"The next one goes between your eyes," François says with a smile.

West's hand on the bottom of my vest shifts, and he taps my back four times.

The hell?

Then I see it. A figure in the shadows. Unsteady, but silent steps.

Zephyr.

Three taps this time.

The woman I love swings a piece of wood up onto her shoulder—her *bare* shoulder. Fuck. She's only wearing a bra and panties, and she's covered in blood.

Two taps.

My Glock lies six inches away, and from this position, the brothers can't see West's other hand.

One tap.

I nod, hoping Zephyr understands what we need her to do.

"Hey, assholes," she says, her voice weak, but steady.

Both brothers turn, startled, and her face, her triumphant smile, is the last thing they see.

West rolls to one side as I grab my Glock, and we fire together.

The leaders of the Strauss Cartel—the men who took my reason to live and tortured her until she could barely walk—fall to the ground, two shots to the head putting an end to both of them.

The piece of wood clatters on the concrete, and Zephyr sways as she tries to take another step. "Ronan? Help."

I race for her, catching her in my arms as she topples over, and she whimpers in pain.

"I'm here, luv. I've got you now."

FIVE BODIES. That's the mess Trevor, Tank, and Raelynn have to clean up. West orders them to pile them all with Oliver, then use some special powder concoction he came up with to start a fire so hot, only their bones will remain.

"It won't spread," he says, handing Tank the keys to the van. "Make sure you're all at least twenty feet away *and* downwind, or you'll never get the stench out of your gear. Once it's burned out, put the bones in the metal storage boxes, then find the gas line to this place. But for fuck's sake, warn us before you set the charge."

"Don't know why you'd want to be clear first. It's cold enough to freeze the tits off a frog in here." With a grin, Raelynn spins on her heel and follows Tank and Trevor to the van while West opens his med kit.

Zephyr passed out seconds after I caught her, and West checks her pulse. "They gave her something. Her heart's racing. I gotta know what it was before I can do anything."

Breaking a packet of smelling salts, he holds it under her nose, and she jerks awake with a shriek. "No! Please!"

I tighten my arms around her, but she claws at me, flailing and catching West in the chin with her bare foot.

"Ronan! Let her go!" he orders, and I do, because no one fucks with West when he uses that tone.

Zephyr crawls away a few feet before she curls into a ball on the floor, whimpering. "No more. No more. No more."

The fear in her voice rips my heart into shreds. "Zephyr? It's Ronan. You're safe now, luv. I'm here."

But she's still whispering "No more" over and over again.

"Zephyr!" West says sharply. "Open your eyes. No one is going to hurt you. I'm a United States Navy SEAL, and you have my word."

Whether West's commanding voice, the combination of words she didn't expect to hear, or something else entirely, Zephyr falls silent, then raises her head. Her eyes are both swollen, and she struggles to focus on him.

"Navy...SEAL?"

"Yes. And that, right there," he jerks his thumb at me, "is a man who loves you and probably wouldn't mind if you let him hold your hand while I examine you."

"Ronan? Oh, God. You're real. I thought..."

I'm at her side in a second and ease her into my arms. Her eyes flutter closed on a sigh. "Zephyr, stay awake, luv. West needs to know what they gave you."

"West? Who's...West?" She's slurring her words, and I wish I could kill those fuckers all over again. Slowly and painfully.

"He's the SEAL. Open your eyes. You have to stay awake now." Taking her hand, I swear under my breath. Her nail beds are dark red. All of them. Deep welts around both wrists ooze blood, and fresh burns mar her stomach. My sleeve—pressed to her back—is sticky with her blood.

"Zephyr." West checks her pulse again, his fingers on her neck as he looks at his watch. "They gave you something. What was it?"

"Amphetamines. Some combo. So I wouldn't pass out." She turns her head toward me. "Can we go home now?"

"Soon, luv. Pay attention to West. He's going to make sure you don't need to go to the hospital." With how bruised and bloody she is, I'm afraid that's exactly where she should be, but hospitals ask questions, and Dax has a private physician on call who's paid enough to keep his mouth shut.

He checks her pupils, asks her how many fingers he's holding up, and if she's had anything to eat or drink.

"N-no food. So thirsty." She's also shivering, and West pulls out a thin, reflective blanket and drapes it over her.

"I'm giving her a sedative to get her heart rate down," he says. "Help her sit up." Rummaging in his kit, he comes away with three pills and a bottle of water. "Diazepam and two ibuprofen. She'll need something stronger for the pain once the stimulants wear off. I'll call Dax from the van and he can have the doc meet you at your place."

"No doctor," she whispers after she swallows the pills and a few sips of water. "No one else. Just you. Please."

Shooting West a questioning glance, I hope he'll agree. Zephyr hates asking for help. Hell, she hates asking for anything.

He frowns. "If she runs a fever, if she can't keep food down, or if she isn't completely lucid in eight hours, I want your word you'll call the doc," West says.

"You have it."

He nods and zips up his kit. "Then let's get out of here so we can burn this place to the ground."

CHAPTER TWENTY-SIX

Zephyr

FROM THE COUCH, I stare out the big picture window at the snow falling steadily over Boston. A fire crackles in the hearth, and I'm wrapped in blankets. I can't get warm, even two full days after Ronan and his team rescued me from that abandoned warehouse twenty miles outside of town.

He spent hours pulling the splinters from my back and shoulders while I bit down on a washcloth so I wouldn't scream. Stitched the worst of the gashes. Then helped me bathe, cleaned and wrapped my wrists, treated my burns, and laid me in his bed.

I thought I'd sleep for a week. But I can't go more than a few hours without a nightmare. They'll fade, as they did before, with time. But until they do, I'm so raw. So tired.

"Zephyr?" Ronan's voice startles me, and I jerk. The blankets are too much pressure on my fingers, and I stifle a whimper of pain. Guilt swims in his eyes, and he curses under his breath. "I'm sorry, luv. I didn't mean to scare you."

"Don't apologize. You did nothing wrong." If I say it enough, maybe he'll start to believe it. He's barely touched me since my very first nightmare, and all I want is for him to hold me.

Setting two cups of tea on the table in front of us, he helps me extricate myself from the layers of wool and fleece. My mug is only half full—my hands are too stiff to hold anything heavy —but the warmth seeping into my fingers feels like heaven. Until Ronan takes his seat at the far end of the couch.

"You can sit next to me." I cup the mug carefully, bringing it to my lips and inhaling the sweet, floral scent of Irish Gold, but he doesn't move. "Ronan, I *need* you to sit next to me. To hold me and tell me you still want me. You *do* still want me, don't you?"

"Shit. Zephyr, I want you so much, I can barely stand it. But I won't be causin' you more pain."

"I'm not suggesting we have wild sex all night long. Yet. Right now, I just want your arms around me."

Ronan closes the distance between us, and I settle against his chest. "If I hurt you—"

"You won't. And you didn't cause any of this." He stiffens at my words, and I cast a glance over my shoulder. "If you'd come in with me, they would have killed you. I'm safe. You and your friends saved my life and cleared my name. I'm free, and that's *all* I care about. That...and you."

We haven't said the words. I want to. But seeing him struggle with his guilt every waking minute has built this wall between us I can't figure out how to tear down.

His phone vibrates, and he checks the screen before he answers. "Ry? You're on speaker."

The former Special Forces team leader has already called twice to tell us how sorry he was he couldn't come to Boston with West and Raelynn, two of the team I now know helped save me.

"Inara and Graham checked in," Ryker says, his voice taking on a satisfied tone I haven't heard before. "Dante Lambert thought he could evade an Army Ranger sniper. He was wrong."

"He's...?" I don't want to say the word. Not over an open line.

"Yup. Niehaus knows the score. He thanked us for cleaning up the mess."

A weight I didn't know I was still carrying lifts, and I set the tea down before I spill it all over myself.

"What about the *other* issue?" Ronan asks.

After a rough chuckle, Ryker clears his throat. "The General Intelligence and Security Service raided three separate safehouses after we pulled all the GPS data off the phones West brought back from the scene. Six arrests, four dead hostiles who weren't smart enough to give up, and the Strauss Cartel will *never* bother you again, Zephyr."

It takes me three tries to manage a "thank you."

"No need for that," Ry says. "No one messes with our family."

He and Ronan say their goodbyes while tears stream down my cheeks. It's over. It's really over.

"Let it out, luv," Ronan whispers in my ear, and I cry until there's nothing left, safe in his arms.

* * *

Ronan

How could I have been so stupid? My misguided attempts to spare Zephyr pain backfired, and I pissed away two days of closeness she *needed*.

No more. I don't know how much time we have together. Now that she's free—truly free—she can go anywhere. Do anything. The idea that she'd stay here with me? It borders on ridiculous.

"I haven't asked," I say quietly. "What will you do now?"

"Do?" She turns to face me, one of her cheeks several shades of purple, and I try not to blame myself all over again.

"You could return to Italy. Or go to Canada. San Diego." I can't meet her gaze for fear of what I'll find in her eyes. "Hawaii."

"Do you *want* me to go somewhere?" Her voice trembles. Shit.

Shock stiffens my shoulders, and I find the courage to look her in the eyes. "Zephyr, I love you. I want you here. With me. For good." A single tear spills onto her cheek, and I dash it away with my thumb. "I should have told you when we found you. Or hell, before I let you walk into that house alone. But I wouldn't blame you for hatin' me."

"Hating you?"

"For takin' so long to get to you. For not bringin' the rest of my team in sooner. For everythin' they did to you." I cup the back of her neck, one of the few places on her body that isn't marred by a fresh wound. "You're my everythin', Zephyr. My family."

It takes her several seconds to find her voice. Seconds I spend in abject terror until she offers me a wobbly smile. "And you're mine. I love you, Ronan. The only place I want to be is with you."

A WEEK LATER, Zephyr's recovered enough to come to Second Sight and meet the rest of the men and women I call family. Easing the brand new leather jacket from her shoulders, I drape it over my arm and open the door.

Thanks to online shopping and a rather large sum of money Wren and Ripper *liberated* from the cartel's various accounts, she has a whole new wardrobe appropriate for winter in

Boston. The soft teal sweater matches her hair, and black jeans mold to her ass. She was giddy over the boots she called "barely practical" and said something under her breath about traction.

"Ronan!" Marjorie hustles around her desk and wraps her arms around me. "Welcome back."

"Uh, thanks." We've never hugged before and it takes me a minute to extricate myself and return my arm to Zephyr's shoulders. "Marjorie, this is Zephyr."

"Oh, honey." Marjorie offers an embrace, but Zephyr shrinks against me, and the office manager's eyes widen. "I'm sorry. I shouldn't have—"

"You don't have to apologize," Zephyr says quietly. "No one but Ronan's touched me in a long time. Unless they were trying to hurt me."

Her openness shocks me, but over the past few days, she's started to relax. To believe that our future together is real.

Marjorie's eyes shimmer, and she presses her hand to her mouth briefly before warmth replaces the sadness written all over her face. "Well, everyone here will make damn sure that never happens again. You're part of the family now. A very welcome addition. Ronan," she nods at me, "hasn't looked this at peace...ever."

Heat licks up my neck, but no one notices, thank God, because Marjorie takes one of her cards from her desk and scribbles something on the back. "If you need *anything*, Zephyr, you call me. Any time. I don't have the skills the others do, but I can bake whatever you can think of, and I've lived in Boston all my life."

"I don't know what to say. Thank you." Zephyr lets me take the card, and when I move to do so, I feel the little flinch in her shoulders.

In most every way, she's recovering. But the few times we've left the apartment, she's been jumpy. Afraid. Always looking around for a member of the cartel or anyone else who might be out to hurt her.

"You're very welcome, honey. The office door is bulletproof, and I see everyone who comes from the elevator and the stairs *long* before they get here."

With one sentence, Marjorie puts Zephyr at ease in a way I never thought to and I mouth, *"Thank you."*

"Now, go on. Everyone's milling about the break room. I'm pretty sure even Dax is out there with them."

Dax anywhere but in his office or in a client meeting is rare, and my eyebrows shoot up. Marjorie leans in and whispers, "You know how he feels about family, Ronan."

I do. Family shows up. Always.

We're halfway down the hall when Dax turns to face us. The rest of the group—Ford and Joey, Trevor and Dani, Clive, Ella, and Tank—gather behind him.

"You work with *all these people*?" Zephyr hisses in my ear.

"Evianna is Dax's wife. You know HomeAssist?" Zephyr nods. "That's her company. She designed the damn thing. And Dani? She's with Trevor. But she's also a reporter for the Boston Globe. The coup in Venezuela last year? That was us. And Dani."

"Oh, my God. I heard about that. *Everyone* heard about that."

Dax clears his throat. "Stop makin' the woman nervous, Ronan." His gentle Southern accent puts folks at ease unless he's in full blown Special Forces mode, and I feel Zephyr settle a little more against me.

After introductions all around, someone—Trevor, I think— offers Zephyr a cup of tea, and Ford shows her around the office. By the time she returns to my side, she's smiling, and some of the light missing from her eyes since her ordeal returns.

Before long I notice Zephyr cradling her right hand in her

left and sticking close to the old wall-mounted radiator, so I wrap my arms around her, being careful not to exert too much pressure on her back. She rests her head on my shoulder with a sigh. "Let me take you home, luv. There's somethin' bein' delivered at five for us, and you're knackered."

"Maybe a little," she admits. "But I can't stay inside forever. Even if a part of me wants to. And, um...Evianna invited us for dinner at the end of the week."

Dinner. With my boss. And his wife. This will either be brilliant or a complete disaster. "We can catch a movie tomorrow. Go out to lunch first. If you want."

"I think I'd like that." Zephyr presses her lips to mine, and suddenly there's a whole other reason I want to get home.

Sweeping my gaze over the family gathered around us, I can't believe how lucky I am. My entire life, I felt like an outsider. But every one of these men and women would risk their lives for me. *Did* risk their lives for me. For the slightest chance to save the woman I love. And they'd do it again.

They rallied around Zephyr this afternoon, welcoming her into the fold without a second thought. And Dax has already told her he, Ry, and Austin are willing to fight for the privilege of having her on their payroll.

Zephyr clasps my hand gingerly, and I bring her knuckles to my lips. "I love you," I whisper against them. "Let's go home."

EPILOGUE

Two Weeks Later

Zephyr

As soon as I step into the apartment, I stop and gape. All the lights are off except for the twinkling multi-colored bulbs on our Christmas tree.

Our tree. The one Ronan had delivered the day I met his Second Sight family.

We picked out the ornaments together. Hung them together. And for the first time in years, I bought presents. My new job—tech consultant and hacker for Austin Pritchard's team and backup for Wren and Ripper as needed—pays more than I thought possible, and I might have gone a little overboard.

Ronan steps out from the hall. Every time I see him, my heart still flutters. He's freshly shaven, and that blue button-up and vest beg to be stripped off his lithe, toned body. "Dinner shows up in half an hour. We've time for a glass of Chardonnay if you'd like." He gestures to the couch where my favorite blanket, an ultra-soft fleece throw in a deep purple, waits for us along with two glasses of wine.

The day after Ronan and his team rescued me, in one of my rambling pain-induced hazes, I told him about the dream I had the day I was taken. Curling up together under a blanket, watching the snow fall. All the lights on the tree, and his whispered *I love you.*

He remembered. All of it.

It's perfect, even if it's not officially Christmas Eve. Tomorrow, we fly out to Seattle with literally everyone else at Second Sight except for Marjorie, Clive, Vazquez, and Ella. Clive's taking care of his mom, Vasquez is spending the holidays with his sister, and Ella...Ronan says she keeps to herself most of the time. I've only met her once, and while she was welcoming and friendly, a part of her seemed so very sad.

I set my bag down on the little table by the door, remove my boots, and pad over to him. "You remembered."

"Every word, luv." He takes my hand, leading me to the couch and then draping the blanket over my legs. Christmas music plays through one of Evianna's HomeAssist units—this one a specially secured model *only* for family—and I look up at Ronan, still convinced this is all a dream. How could I have found such a perfect, wonderful, kind man while on the run and wanted for murder? Why did he ever take a chance on me?

Because I needed a family. And Ronan needed to remember he'd found one.

After we toast, Ronan pulls a small box from behind a throw pillow. "This isn't exactly a Christmas gift, luv. It already belongs to you. But when you see it, I think you'll understand why I waited."

My hands tremble as I tug on the ribbon. "My papa's ring!" I hadn't seen it since I left it for Ronan, hoping he'd know to find me.

"Your hands were sore for so long. I worried wearin' it

would bring you more pain than peace. But after last night..."

He grins, and my cheeks flush hot. We had some rather... intense sex the previous evening where we both used our hands to their fullest.

Sliding the ring onto my thumb, I admire it in the flickering light from our tree and the warm glow from the hearth.

Ronan wraps his arm around my shoulders so I can lean against him. "This is our first Christmas as a family. The one with just you and me, *and* the one we'll have out in Seattle. I thought...you might want somethin' from your father with you for the celebrations."

Snuggling closer, I tip my head up to kiss him. He no longer asks me to believe or trust for a single moment. I've strung each one—every moment I saved up in my mind and heart—together into what I hope will be a lifetime of love and trust with this man.

He's my home. The missing piece to my heart and soul. The man who took a chance on me when I was broken, alone, and determined not to let anyone in.

"I'd forgotten how to love," I whisper against his neck, and his lips skim the shell of my ear, a gesture so tender, I melt every single time. "Until you reminded me."

"You didn't need remindin', luv. Just someone to believe in you."

Here, in the warmth of a home I never thought I'd find, we lose ourselves in one another. Two loners who will never be alone again.

***

Thank you for reading *Protecting His Target*. Every time I finish one of the *Away From Keyboard* or *Gone Rogue* books, I swear the characters are my new favorites. Because they are. Every single couple has a special place in my heart—and always will.

Ronan and Zephyr? They were hard to get to know. Ronan

was pissed off most of the time, and Zephyr hadn't trusted anyone in so long, she *definitely* wasn't going to trust me.

At least not at first. It took a while. But once they opened up...it was like neither of them wanted to stop talking.

In the end, their story made me laugh and cry, and I hope you felt the same.

Next up? Rogue Survivor. This is Connor's book. He's Quinton's brother, and if you read Braving His Past, you know he has *a long way to go* for his redemption. I hope you'll preorder Rogue Survivor now!

After that? Defending His Hope.

Love,

Patricia

ACKNOWLEDGMENTS

Writing is a solitary affair. Most of the time, it's just me and my computer (or notebook). I don't often put acknowledgements in a book because...honestly...I'd just thank the same people over and over again for the exact same things.

Also, I don't even know how many people read acknowledgements.

But after being diagnosed with several autoimmune conditions, losing Binky, and the general stress of 2020 and 2021, I needed a little more help than usual on Rogue Officer and Protecting His Target.

I want to thank Lauren for all of her encouragement. She was a constant source of positive energy for me, and helped me finesse a few parts of this book that are so much better for her having touched them.

As always, I want to thank my editor, Jayne, and my proofreader, Sam. As well as my BFF, Jill, who gets some of the most ridiculous text messages from me and still hasn't told me to get lost.

Lastly, I want to thank everyone who's read this far. Authors do what we do because we love to tell stories. But without read-ers, we'd end up keeping all these stories to ourselves. Thank you to everyone who purchased Protecting His Target or checked it out from a library. You rock, and I love all of you.

ABOUT THE AUTHOR

Patricia D. Eddy writes romance for the beautifully broken. Fueled by coffee, wine, and Doctor Who episodes on repeat, she brings damaged heroes and heroines together to find their happy ever afters in many different worlds. From military to paranormal to BDSM, her characters are unstoppable forces colliding with such heat, sparks always fly.

Patricia makes her home in Seattle with her husband and very spoiled cats, and when she's not writing, she loves working on home improvement projects, especially if they involve power tools.

Her award-winning *Away From Keyboard* series will always be her first love, because that's where she realized the characters in her head were telling their own stories—and she was just writing them down.

You can reach Patricia all over the web...
patriciadeddy.com
patricia@patriciadeddy.com

facebook.com/patriciadeddyauthor
twitter.com/patriciadeddy
instagram.com/patriciadeddy
bookbub.com/profile/patricia-d-eddy

ALSO BY PATRICIA D. EDDY

Away From Keyboard

Dive into a steamy mix of geekery and military prowess with the men and women of Hidden Agenda and Second Sight.

Breaking His Code

In Her Sights

On His Six

Second Sight

By Lethal Force

Fighting For Valor

Finding Their Forevers (a holiday short story)

Call Sign: Redemption

Braving His Past

Protecting His Target

Defending His Hope

Gone Rogue (an Away From Keyboard spinoff series)

Rogue Protector

Rogue Officer

Rogue Survivor

Dark PNR

These novellas will take you into the darker side of the paranormal with vampires, witches, angels, demons, and more.

Forever Kept

Immortal Hunter

Wicked Omens

Storm of Sin

By the Fates

Check out the COMPLETE By the Fates series if you love dark and steamy tales of witches, devils, and an epic battle between good and evil.

By the Fates, Freed

Destined: A By the Fates Story

By the Fates, Fought

By the Fates, Fulfilled

In Blood

If you love hot Italian vampires and and a human who can hold her own against beings far stronger, then the In Blood series is for you.

Secrets in Blood

Revelations in Blood

Holidays and Heroes

Beauty isn't only skin deep and not all scars heal. Come swoon over sexy vets and the men and women who love them.

Mistletoe and Mochas

Love and Libations

Restrained

Do you like to be tied up? Or read about characters who do? Enjoy a fresh COMPLETE BDSM series that will leave you begging for more.

In His Silks

Christmas Silks

All Tied Up For New Year's

In His Collar

9 781942 258421